STORMBRINGER

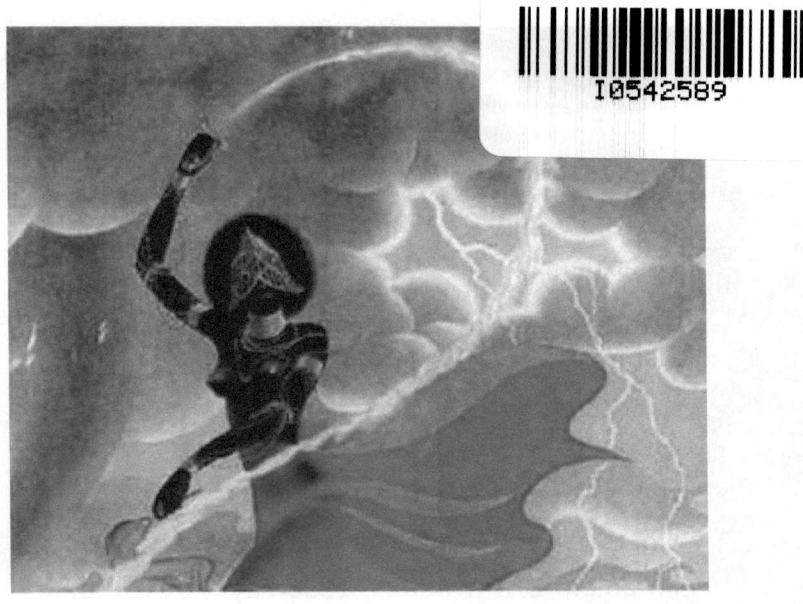

An Orisha Rising Novel

By Tai Daniels

Paradigm/SHIFT Books

Atlanta, GA

STORMBRINGER

STORMBRINGER

BOOKS BY TIFFANY M. DAVIS

The Bastille Family Chronicles series
The Bastille Family Chronicles: Camille
The Bastille Family Chronicles: Dominic
The Bastille Family Chronicles: Nicollette (2016)

The Sebastian Scott novels (written as Tee Emdee)
Blizzard

The Orisha Rising series (written as Tai Daniels)
Stormbringer
Ironborn (2016)

SHOUTOUTS, THANX, &
ACKNOWLEDGEMENTS

As always, special thanks to Corregan G. Brown.

Thanks to my Twitter Tribe advance reading team (Parrish, CG, Sterling, Rod) for spreading the word. #DiverseSFF

A special thanks and acknowledgment to those practitioners of Yoruba-based beliefs, including *vodun* (voodoo), Santería, Lukúmi/Lucúmi, and Palo Mayombe (Las Reglas de Colombo). Shoutout to Sephrena of Tribe of the Sun, for patiently answering my questions.

The above religions tend to overlap with regard to legend and identification of the *orisha*. As is usually the case when there are different paths, there are variations on practices. I tried to stay as true as I could to the most basic and commonly agreed-upon attributes of the *orisha*. Any liberties taken in this novel are mine, and mine alone.

To the *orisha*: I hope that you are pleased.

STORMBRINGER

STORMBRINGER

PROLOGUE

Once upon a time, the orisha, *the African deities, ruled. Olodumare, The Supreme Creator, wept her tears and created a world in which the* orisha *loved, fought, and lived. Their pleasures were great, as were their appetites; their pain, relatively little. They faithfully tended the domains and dominions for which they bore gifts, and their world flourished. Life was good.*

Then Olodumare created humans. The orisha *were curious about these fragile beings with finite life spans. Curiosity gave way to amusement as they saw how awed the humans were by their powers. Amusement soon gave way to arrogance, for who does not enjoy being worshipped and adored? Adulation gave way to communion of a more intimate nature between the* orisha *and the humans; the* orisha *were pleased to discover beings that weren't used to their unbridled lust, and the humans couldn't get enough of the pleasure bestowed by the* orisha. *Soon, the first wave of human children borne of the* orisha *came.*

Not all were pleased at these unions. It was the opinion of some orisha *that these* demigod children were little more than abominations. Even worse, what if they manifested powers? The world of the orisha was cutthroat enough; why add more competition? The defenders of these children countered that they were conceived in love (or as close to it as an orisha could get) and deserved the chance to live; after all, didn't the orisha, as a whole, revere life and the process that created it?

The debates raged until Olodumare, in her guise as Olorun, the wise father (the second of her three manifestations), came to compromise. The lives of these children would be spared, but they would be sent to Earth to live their lives as regular humans, separate from the deities. As for the manifestation of powers, well...no one really knew for sure if that would occur--not even Orunmila the Great Diviner could see their future in his cowrie shells--so that issue would be addressed if and when it came to pass.

The solution barely appeased both sides, but they deferred to Olorun's judgment. The children were sent to earth as infants and were placed under the protection of those who served their parents. These children became known as the omo ṣọnu olorun, the Lost Children of the Gods.

As time passed, the orisha *noticed that the Lost Children were like other humans, except that they had longer lives; some even had a bit of a boost to their usual talents, but nothing that would land them on the covers of the silly tabloids that humans loved so much. They relaxed their monitoring of the Lost Children and decided that they were no longer a threat to the* orisha *and their omniverse.*

The descendants of the Lost Children, however, were another matter...

STORMBRINGER

****ONE****

My footsteps became heavy as I entered the last mile of my usual weekend hike through the forest. I liked the solo outings; they not only kept me close to nature, but allowed me to get in some much-needed thinking time. My day job in the Development Department of a local museum (the place where we generate all those give-us-money missives) sucked all of the energy out of me; it was only when I got outside that I felt unfettered and free.

I looked up at the tops of the pine trees that surrounded me and inhaled their astringent scent. I was so busy admiring the view above that I failed to pay attention to the path in front of me. My foot came down upon a large rock and my ankle rolled...as did the rest of me, right down a hill into the deeper floor of the forest. I finally tumbled into the base of one of the trees I so liked to look at; my head cracked against the rough bark hard enough to make me see stars. I lay there to get my bearings, and then sat up slowly. A quick sweep of my hand around my aching head didn't yield any blood, so I hadn't cracked my hard head open; a possible concussion, however, was another matter. The shift to a sitting position sparked a new round of pain in my already throbbing ankle, and I worked my right hiking boot and sock off to assess the damage. My ankle, which was rather slim for my six-foot height, was now roughly the size of one of those value rolls of ground beef sold in grocery stores. I still had a mile to go to get back to my car; what would have been about a half-hour walk might now take two to three times that.

"Damn it," I hissed to myself as I balled my fists in angry frustration. Had I been paying more attention, I wouldn't be in this predicament. As if in agreement, the sky rumbled and I looked up to see thunderclouds rolling in. Funny, the day had been clear and sunny, and there was no forecast for rain through the end of the week. A sharp crack rent the air, and lightning zigzagged through one of the larger clouds. On top of everything else, I was going to get rain-soaked if I didn't hurry up and get back to my car. My day was just getting better and better.

Another quick check showed that I hadn't broken anything, and that my head and ankle were the main issues. I looked at the steep incline to my left, then ahead of me to where there was no true path. There were spots here

and there with no trees, but nothing that I could
see to lead me back to the main hiking trail
above. I'd have to climb back up the incline, on
one leg.

I looked back at the incline again, noting
the lack of exposed root systems or even
makeshift handholds, trying to figure out how I
was going to haul myself upward. I examined my
fingernails, which I usually kept cut short; no
help there. I might have to call an ambulance, or
at least the park office. I pulled my cell phone
out of the inner pocket of my Gore-Tex jacket
and saw a circle with a slash across it instead of
the bars I'd hoped for. No signal at all. Movement
in the corner of my eye snapped my head
around, which stoked the headache that had
been fading away. A man stood there, another
hiker from the looks of things. He was dressed in
jeans and a red-and-black plaid flannel shirt,
worn under a black fleece vest. A large red
backpack was on his back, and he carried a long,
black cane. I hadn't even heard him approach.

"Oh! Hello," I greeted with caution. "I
didn't see you there." It was not unheard of for
the homeless to make camp in the woods,
though this man looked too well-kempt. Still,

getting jacked in the middle of the woods was not on the agenda.

"I'm hard to see sometimes," the man replied. His black, button eyes examined me with curiosity. "Did you hurt yourself?"

"Yeah, I twisted my ankle on a rock and fell off the trail up there." I gestured to the top of the incline. "I'm trying to figure how to get back up. Do you know of another trail that can lead from here, back to the main trail?"

"I know many paths," the man said. His speech had an interesting pattern, like English wasn't his first language. A dimple in his bearded cheek twitched with suppressed amusement, which gave me pause because there was nothing funny about my situation.

"Great. If you could just point me in the right direction, I'd appreciate it. Or, do you have a cell phone that gets a signal? I may need to call an ambulance or something to help me out of here."

The man leaned on his cane, his long, elegant brown fingers folded atop the head, which upon closer inspection was shaped like the head of a twining snake. "Any direction is wrong if you are not going where you need to be."

"Excuse me?" My head hurt, my ankle was killing me, and this man wanted to talk like a bootleg fortune cookie?

"You have not yet learned where you need to go. But I can help show you, with the proper tokens of appreciation."

I sighed aloud. Of course this dude would hit me up for money while I'm down. People didn't do much out of the kindness of their hearts anymore. "I don't have any cash on me, but once we're back to the main trail, I can go to the ATM in the gift shop, and..."

The man chuckled. "If it is assistance you seek, I can provide it. But you must pay homage."

"I just told you, I don't have any cash on me. But if you can get me to the ATM machine, I will..."

"Do you smoke?"

The sudden switch in subject confused me. "What?"

"Do you smoke?" the man repeated.

"Uh, no."

Disappointment crossed his face; his unlined dark brown skin put his age anywhere from thirty to seventy. Only the glints of silver in his beard and in the edges of tightly coiled hair peeking beneath his red knitted cap tilted his age toward the upward end of that spectrum. "I could really use a cigarette right about now," he mused. "Or a cigar. A nice, fat Cohiba, or maybe a Monte Cristo." He stared at me thoughtfully. "Got any candy?"

I reached into my pocket and pulled out a half-eaten roll of butter rum LifeSavers. I held them out to the man, who snatched them eagerly. He held the partial roll up to his wide nostrils and inhaled deeply in appreciation before popping one into his mouth. "Delicious," he pronounced with a smack of his lips. "I will get you the help you need." Then he disappeared.

I stared in shock at the spot where the man once stood. I must have hit my head harder than I'd thought; surely hallucinations were a sign of concussion? Well, I'd have to go back to my original plan of hauling myself up the steep incline. At least I only lost some LifeSavers. I reached back into my pocket where the candy used to be; since I seem to be hallucinating, it's possible that the candy fell out of my pocket as I rolled down the incline. It didn't disappear with a phantom man who really wanted a smoke.

There was a rustle in the trees near me, then another man walked out. Or rather, limped, as he walked with the assistance of a long, wooden staff with a lot of carvings all over it. Unlike his counterpart, he wore a deep brown suede coat with cream-colored shearling lining and trim, to match his boots. The hood of the coat was pulled over his head and partially obscured his eyes. He came over to me and looked down, only his full lips and part of his wide nose visible beneath the hood. "You are injured," he said. His voice held the rustle of the wind through the trees.

"I hurt my ankle and head when I fell down the incline."

"Let me see." He knelt with some difficulty and placed a large hand, covered with healed chicken pox scars, on my swollen ankle. I felt a rush of heat, then tingling, and the swelling and pain went away. He removed his hand and my ankle looked just as it did that morning, when I pulled a sock over it. Before I could fully process what happened, he reached both hands out and placed them atop my head. Again, the intense heat and tingling, and my headache was gone.

I rose and stood on both feet, testing my ankle. It was back to normal. "Thank you," I stammered as I bent to put back on my sock and boot. "But how...who..."

The man didn't speak, merely nodded his head and faded back into the woods. I got myself together and scrambled back up the incline and hightailed it back to my car.

***

Babalúayé limped through the woods to a spot invisible to the human eye. He approached the shimmery space and touched it; the shimmer solidified into an oval that opened onto an arrangement of scattered, thatched-roof huts sitting atop packed red earth. He stepped through with care and entered an African village that was home to the *orisha*. The dusty streets were neat, and he nodded greetings to the robed passersby. He approached a large, elegant hut with triple-thatched roofs and an open-air construction. He ducked beneath the main entrance and approached the dais. He set his staff aside and knelt with care before the white-robed figure sitting in a palm frond throne. "*Baba*," he greeted with a bowed head.

Olorun inclined his head to return the greeting. "Babalúayé."

"Are you not going to greet me?" Eshú, draped in red robes, said from his place to the side of the dais. He polished his long, dark cane, taking special care with the snake on the head of it.

Babalúayé shot him a droll look. "Should I thank you for making more work for me today? If Erinle was not keeping an eye on a potential tsunami near Malaysia, and Osain was not inspiring a scientist to 'discover' a new species of plant, I wouldn't be here. You are fortunate that I had some time since I got the Ebola outbreak in Sierra Leone under control." Eshú stuck out his tongue. Babalúayé turned his attention back to Olorun. "*Baba*, I have news. I have found one of the *omo sǫnu olorun*."

"The Lost Children of the Gods? Truly?" Olorun sat up with interest, the silver embroidery on his robes twinkling in the rays of sun that shot through the front door. "Where?"

"In the forest. A human girl--well, a woman, I suppose--hurt herself in a fall. Eshú called me to heal her. She would have a hard time making her way back to the main trail, otherwise. She had a badly sprained ankle and a concussion."

"I knew I felt it," Eshú added. "But I wanted to make sure. I was glad that she had injuries that needed tending."

"Tell me, Babalúayé; whose child is she?"

Babalúayé and Eshú looked at each other before Babalúayé answered. "I suspect she is Changó's child."

"There have long been rumors, *Baba*," Eshú murmured as Olorun raised an eyebrow.

Babalúayé nodded in agreement. "The woman made the thunder roll with a simple spark of frustration, and she had fortitude of spirit that I usually associate with Changó. Lightning flared as well, but did not strike. She is unaware of what she can do."

"If she brought lightning as well, then she could also be Oyá's child," Olorun pointed out. "Where lightning goes, thunder is sure to follow. But if that were the case, the child would be an *orisha* herself. The Ibeji are the sacred twins of Changó and Oshun, not to mention the children that Erinle fathered with Oshun."

"So either Changó or Oyá is her parent," Babalúayé countered.

"There is another option." Babalúayé and Olorun looked at Eshú. "Both Changó and Oyá each had a liaison with a human, and those humans produced this woman."

Babalúayé nodded thoughtfully. "That is the most logical conclusion, since the woman is human and not *orisha*."

"She was born and raised among the humans, as she should have been. This may have protected her to an extent of which she is not aware." Olorun sat back in his throne chair with a thoughtful look. "How is this possible, that a human would have the powers of an *orisha*? Especially a human who had not had direct contact with us." Another thought came to him, and he sighed. "After all this time, Oshun does not know about her. She would be devastated."

"Especially if the child is a direct descendant of Oyá and Changó," Eshú commented.

Olorun nodded at this truth. Oyá and Changó began their affair shortly after his marriage to Oshun, and she soon became his second wife. Oshun never forgave either of them. If she knew a child of their human dalliances existed... "Does she have protection in the human realm?"

"She does, *Baba*," Eshú reassured him. "Since the day she was born."

"Good. How old is the woman?"

"She just turned thirty-six in human years, *Baba*."

"A multiple of nine," Olorun murmured. "Indeed, she is too young to be one of the Lost

Children, though I am sometimes unaware of the passage of time in the human realm. Yes, she is a descendant of Oyá; nine is Oyá's sacred number." He sighed heavily and fingered the silver trim of his robe. "We will need to make sure that she is trained properly as her powers manifest."

"Do you think she will have more powers, *Baba*?" Babalúayé asked in surprise. "The woman is rather old for them to manifest."

"She is likely a direct descendant of Oyá and Changó, and they both rule different aspects of storms. Storms are unpredictable. We should be prepared, as should she."

Babalúayé bowed his head. "As you command, *Baba*."

Outside the hut, a rattlesnake moved from its coiled position beneath a window and slithered into the nearby grasses. Soon it arrived to a large metal hut from which great quantities of heat emitted. Ogún was bent over a red-hot sword, his sweat-sheened muscles rippling with every blow of his hammer against the heated metal atop the anvil. The snake entered the hut via a space beneath a metal cabinet where the *orisha*'s tools were stored. The snake rattled its tail in greeting.

Ogún turned at the sound and stared at the snake. The snake raised its upper body; reptile and *orisha* communed as the snake hissed every detail of the meeting between The Creator, The Messenger Trickster, and The Healer. "Thank you, friend," Ogún rumbled in a bass voice when the snake had finished its recital. The snake dipped its head in acknowledgement and slithered off into the large area of farmed land behind the hut.

Ogún turned back to the machete on his workbench as he considered the snake's tale. So, that Changó once had a human consort, as did Oyá. How fitting for him to rut like the dog that he was, with a human whore; Oyá was no better. And Oshun, that dear, sweet, soul, had no clue. Ogún finished shaping the machete and used a pair of large, blackened tongs to dip it in a tub of cool water. Steam rose from the tub; the hissing sound was similar to that of the snake just moments ago, and not unlike the movement of the sacred palm fronds belted around his waist. He placed the cooling machete on a wire rack to complete its hardening and began to clean up, even as he pondered his course of action regarding this human scion of Changó and Oyá.

Perhaps Oshun should know; while Ogún didn't want to cause her any further pain, he also saw it as a good way to get back at Changó for his arrogant, womanizing ways. And as for Oyá, what better pain to inflict than the death of her own lineage? A stab of pain shot through his barreled chest. He would have gladly given his former wife a dozen children; she had only to ask. The fact that the one child she did have was with a human descendant of Changó was insult to injury. It just confirmed that he, Ogún, was right to join the push for the human consorts to be banished to earth, so many years ago. Such relationships with humans were abominations and their descendants even more so.

Ogún finished straightening his hut. He needed to inform Oshun before she learned of this through unsavory channels. And he would carry out whatever actions she deemed prudent in this matter. It was the least he could do for her.

***

Aganjú strode toward the crowd near the shoreline, his majestic brow furrowed with concern. The waves crested high and blue, and some humans dotted the seas on these silly contraptions called surfboards, which they used to ride the waves. He snorted; they had only his wife, Yemajá, to thank for not meeting an untimely end in those strong waters. She was much too kind to beings who often did not give her proper homage. He let the sun beam down upon his bald, brown head as the sea breezes caressed his cheek. Hawai'i was a compromise for them both; he didn't care much for water, but Yemajá didn't care for the desert, his preferred home. In this place she could have her vast ocean, and he could live among the volcanoes that dotted the Hawaiian Islands, and they could be together without much strife.

Aganjú knew where he would find his wife today. She would be watching a contest of humans, who competed with each other to see who could best the strong waves of the Pacific Ocean on those silly surfboards. These contests had grown in popularity over the decades, especially due to the moving pictures called *Point Break* and *Blue Crush*. The winners of these contests won a lot of money and had their likenesses and names used to sell all sorts of things that humans deemed important, from clothing to hygiene products, in an attempt to gain glory by proxy. He approached the large crowd and used his sizeable bulk to slip through the throng of people. For most humans, they only felt a slight disturbance of air that could easily be mistaken for the tropical breeze, and he was as visible as he chose. He saw Yemajá in human form, sitting in a bright blue beach chair with a large blue and white beach umbrella to shield her from the sun. Blue-framed sunglasses perched on her nose while seashell earrings dangled from her ears and swayed in tune to her periodic clapping and cheering.

"I knew you'd be by soon," Yemajá said as she added to the applause. At Aganjú's inquiring look she nodded her head in the direction of the volcano Kilauea, where rivers of glowing red lava flowed from its mouth, and were visible from even this great distance. "It has been particularly active today. What troubles you, my love?"

Aganjú adjusted his knee-length, dark denim shorts as he sat in the empty blue beach chair that had materialized beside Yemajá. His muscular chest rippled beneath his orange-red T-shirt with a large yellow appliqué of the sun in its center. "Have you heard? A descendant of the *omo sọnu olorun* has been found."

"Oh?" Yemajá shot Aganjú a surprised look before turning her attention back to the

23

contest. The crowd gave a collective gasp as a surfer went down beneath the large curl of a wave and disappeared for over ten seconds. Yemajá waved a hand, causing her blue crystal bracelet to twinkle in the sun. The surfer popped to the surface like a cork. His surfboard did as well, though it was now in two pieces. The crowd cheered with relief as a contest lifeguard rode out to the surfer on a Jet Ski and towed him--and his broken board--back to shore. Yemajá sat back with a satisfied smirk on her face and looked at Aganjú. "Where is this descendant?"

"In a place called Atlanta, Georgia."

"Who are her parents?"

Aganjú hesitated, then sighed. "I do not know for sure, but they had to have consorted with Changó and Oyá."

Yemajá's good mood evaporated. "This is known for certain?"

Aganjú explained how Eshú found the girl--a woman, really--in a forest, and how Babalúayé healed her injuries from a fall.

Yemajá shook her head, all interest in the surfing contest gone. "Oshun's wrath will level the heavens."

"She is still no match for her sister Oyá. Speaking of which...apparently, this human woman can bring the storms. She caused the skies to shake out of frustration."

"What more can be expected from a progeny of storm *orisha*?" Yemajá played with one of her earrings as she ruminated. "The child is under protection?"

"As far as I know. Though once Oshun finds out, that protection will be short-lived."

"Yes," Yemajá nodded. "She has many allies among the *orisha*, plus her human worshippers." She sighed. "Needless to say, Ogún will be in the midst of things."

"Right at Oshun's side," Aganjú agreed. "He never really got over her. She was there for him when Oyá left him for Changó."

"Love--as well as lust--is an extremely powerful force, as well Oshun knows." She looked around at the dispersing crowd in surprise; she hadn't even noticed that the contest was over. She looked over to where the winner posed for cameras. "Where is our son?"

"I have no idea where Changó is. He is not in the village, or else Ogún would have tried to kill him by now."

"Then we must find him and warn him. And before I deal with my youngest sister Oshun, I must deal with Oyá the elder. She needs to

know that her lineage is in danger." Yemajá
stood and snapped her fingers; the beach chairs
and umbrella disappeared.

Aganjú struggled to his feet from where
he'd been unceremoniously dumped in the sand
when his chair disappeared. "I wish you'd give
me fair warning when you do that," he grumbled
as he dusted sand from his backside.

"Aww, poor baby. I'll kiss it better later."
Yemajá's eyes danced with mirth as she linked
her arm through Aganjú's. "First, let's try to stop
an *orisha* war."

✳✳TWO✳✳

The tinkling of tombstone-shaped copper chimes over the door announced my entrance to The Eggplant. The store's registered name was Susan's Spiritual Shoppe, but it had been called "The Eggplant" by locals for almost the entirety of the shop's thirty-year existence--no mean feat, since the area in which it was located had transformed into a shopping and entertainment hub over the past five years, bringing the requisite sky-high rents. The dark purple-hued interior was strangely soothing, along with the sandalwood-infused incense blend that constantly burned. A few people milled about, flipping through books or trying to divine their futures by throwing the display model of cowrie shells. I made a point to try and visit the store at least once a week; the store just drew me in, for some reason.

I lingered by a new display of books on female African warriors and tucked a copy under my arm for purchase. I went over to the jewelry display, which contained both commercially manufactured and hand-crafted items from local artisans, sold on consignment. As I checked for new inventory, I felt a presence behind me. I turned and saw Navasha, the shop's current owner and the niece of the founder, Susan. "How do you do that?" I asked as my heart rate returned to normal. "You're like a cat. I'm going to get you some bells."

Navasha laughed, causing the lightning-shaped pendant on her necklace to glint in the overhead fluorescent lights. "I hear that a lot. Anyway, what have you been up to, Violet?"

"Nothing much. Same old, same old."

"Been hiking lately?"

"Yeah." I decided not to mention the weird men in the woods.

Navasha went around to the other side of the glass jewelry case. Her waist-length gray dreadlocks swayed beneath the wide purple scarf that held them back from her unlined brown face. "I made something with you in mind. I think you'd like it." Navasha made copper and raw gemstone jewelry that sold well.

She removed a copper necklace from which little lightning-shaped charms dangled between alternating cabochon amethysts and garnets. It wasn't really my style, but it appealed to me. The door chimes tinkled again and a military man in a camouflaged uniform entered the shop. His uniform pants were tucked neatly into his combat boots; the insignia on his sleeves and cap indicated that he had a bit of rank, but not much. He removed his cap, revealing low-cut hair; and his sunglasses, revealing cool grey eyes. He nodded at me and Navasha before sauntering past. He made a beeline for a display of masked warrior women in torn rag skirts.

"Go ahead; try it on."

I fastened the necklace at the nape of my neck. It settled across my collarbones and felt strangely warm, in contrast to the metal's coolness when I took it from Navasha's hand. I leaned into the standing mirror that graced the top of the jewelry case, turning my neck this way and that to admire the effect. Again, not something I'd normally wear, but it felt nice around my neck. "I like it. How much?"

Navasha merely smiled. "It's a gift."

"Navasha, I can't not pay for this," I protested. "This is a nice piece of craftsmanship."

"Take it. It looks good on you."

"But..."

"No buts." She relocked the jewelry case; the lock tumbler slid home with a click of finality. "Please accept it. It'll make me feel better."

Her wink belied the undercurrent of urgency in her voice. I didn't understand it, but shrugged it off. "Well, thank you, Navasha. I really appreciate it. It's great."

"You're welcome."

I gave her a hug, paid for my book, and walked out of the store. I enjoyed the feel of the sun on my head as I strolled down the street amid the light crowd and window-shopped at the establishments I passed. I turned down a side street where I'd parked my car. Halfway down the block I heard heavy footsteps; I looked over my shoulder and saw the officer that had been in The Eggplant. I arrived at my car and had just unlocked the doors with my key fob when a hard shove sent me sprawling onto the cracked concrete. The bag with my book went flying as my palms and denim-covered knees scraped against the sidewalk. I tried to get up but a kick sent me back to the ground. My side exploded with pain and I could barely catch my breath. I managed to roll to my side just as the soldier came close enough for me to smell the polish on his boots. "What...why..." I panted. Thunder rumbled in the distance.

"Die, Stormbringer," the soldier snarled as he pulled a wicked-looking knife out of the large pocket on his thigh.

I tossed up a hand in a pitiful attempt to shield myself from the coming blow. Heat enveloped my hand and a flash of light shot out of it. The man blew backward and landed on his back with a grunt, and did not move any more. The knife clattered from his hand and rolled off the curb and beneath another parked car.

***

Eshú rushed into Olorun's hut, ignoring protocol. Olorun looked up in surprise from his snack of *fufu* and spicy soup. "It has begun, *Baba*," he panted as he leaned against a nearby table to catch his breath.

"What? What has begun?"

"A war, *Baba*. The descendant of the *omo sọnu olorun* was attacked in broad daylight."

Olorun dropped the soup-soaked *fufu* that had been en route to his lips. The ball of pounded yam tumbled off the table and onto the floor. "A war?" he whispered. "But how? Who knew of her existence except me, you, and Babalúayé?" His tone turned accusatory. "Did you tell anyone else?"

"I may have mentioned it to Aganjú," Eshú admitted, "who probably told Yemajá, and either one or both probably told Changó, or will soon."

Olorun shook his head. "No. Even if Changó knew, he would not attack the woman. He'd be too intrigued by a human of his lineage, and a female at that. No, this was done by an enemy of either Changó, or Oyá, or both." He closed his eyes; seconds later, Babalúayé appeared.

"Yes, *Baba*?" He leaned heavily on his wooden staff, carved with symbols of healing.

"It has come to my attention that Aganjú and Yemajá are aware of the woman, thanks to Eshú." Eshú gave a sheepish grin. "Have you mentioned her existence to anyone else?"

"No, *Baba*." Babalúayé's expression was noncommittal as he adjusted his brown robes. "I prefer my own company." Indeed, his was a solitary existence.

"Then we need to figure out who would want to harm the woman."

"That is not difficult, *Baba*," Babalúayé said. "One has only to look to her lineage to determine her most immediate threats. There is also the question of timing; whoever attacked her feels the need to move quickly. There is a question in that, as well."

Eshú and Olorun stared at each other as two names came to mind. "Oshun and Ogún," Eshú nodded, a grim expression on his face.

"Or even Oba," Olorun added. "Despite her meek nature, she is not to be underestimated. And she has good reason to despise both Changó and Oyá."

Neither Eshú nor Olorun could forget Oba's wails of physical pain when she cut off her ear and served it to Changó in a soup, in a desperate attempt to keep his eyes from straying. Her emotional wails when he left her for Oshun, and later took up with Oyá, were even more profound. Though she and Changó were still married, it was in name only; he never returned to her as her true husband and she continued to live as a single woman in the outskirts of the village. Oba also harbored deep resentment against Oshun and Oyá, the two women who took--and kept--away the only man she'd ever loved.

"We cannot rule out Ogún, *Baba*." Eshú sat cross-legged on a mat of woven palm fronds and removed a pouch of tobacco and a dried palm leaf from his jacket pocket. He rolled a homemade cigarette and lit it with a snap of his fingers; the aromatic odor of tobacco soon filled the hut.

Olorun pondered this, then nodded. "True. He would gladly protect Oshun from that which he deemed harmful."

"But how would he know? The only ones in this hut when we discovered the woman were you, myself, and Babalúayé, and I only mentioned the woman to Aganjú two days ago."

"Do not forget that Ogún has dominion over rattlesnakes, hawks, panthers, dogs, and wolves. It would not be difficult for him to obtain information that we try to keep secret. In which case, we will need to act quickly. If he has indeed gleaned the particulars of his meeting, then chances are that he is on his way to inform Oshun, if he hasn't already." Olorun rose and gathered his gold-shot white robes. "We must prepare."

"For what, *Baba*?" Eshú followed him to another room of the hut. Babalúayé limped behind them.

"A war."

***

Ogún arrived at the posh offices of Golden River Staffing, in a luxury business tower in the affluent Buckhead area of Atlanta. He adjusted his glasses and tucked the roll of engineering blueprints beneath his arm before approaching the receptionist's desk. "Good afternoon," he greeted. "I'm from Ironworks Engineering, ma'am, to see the boss."

The receptionist frowned and checked the appointment calendar on her computer. "Did you have an appointment, sir?"

"No, but this is an urgent matter regarding the foundation of your building." While this was not true in the literal sense--the building had been well constructed by humans who served him--it was true in the figurative sense. This news would shake up everything that Oshun thought about her world, and the world of the *orisha*.

The receptionist picked up the desk phone and pressed a button. After a brief, murmured conversation, she hung up. "You can go right back," she said in surprise. "Last door on the right."

Ogún nodded his thanks and walked through the glass double doors behind the receptionist's desk that led to the offices. Attractive people--male and female--bustled about doing business-related tasks, their expressions as serious as their business casual attire. One would never know that this was one of the largest upscale escort services in the country. Politicians, celebrities, and other wealthy men and women kept business booming.

The nickels tucked in the fronts Ogún's loafers glinted beneath the overhead lights as he strode down the thickly carpeted hallway toward Oshun's office. When he arrived, the *orisha* herself was seated behind a large wooden desk, her head bent over a stack of papers. She smiled when Ogún stepped through the doorway, and scooped a lock of her dark, shoulder-length hair behind one ear. Citrine-studded golden pearls winked from her earlobes.

"Ogún! To what do I owe this pleasant surprise?" She rose and walked around the desk, the slit in her fitted black skirt revealing a healthy glimpse of brown thigh encased in sheer black, lace-topped thigh-high stockings. The vee neckline of her yellow wrap silk blouse was low enough to show a glimpse of generous cleavage peeking out of a metallic gold lace bra. The blouse was fastened at her hip with a jeweled pin in the shape of a peacock.

Ogún accepted her embrace, the scent of her perfume stirring his loins. "I had to see you."

Oshun checked her dainty gold watch. "Well, I have a meeting in half an hour, but I can always make time for you. We can make it quick." A dimple flashed in her cheek as she reached for the silver buckle on Ogún's belt.

As much as Ogún wanted to lie with Oshun again, there were more pressing matters. He stayed her hand. "That is not why I'm here, Oshun."

"Oh?" She moved her hand up to his broad chest and adjusted the collar of his dark green shirt.

"We must talk about the *omo sọnu olorun.*"

"The Lost Children? But why?"

"Perhaps we should sit." He led her over to a loveseat against an adjacent wall. Oshun sank onto the yellow and white-patterned fabric and crossed her legs, revealing a flash of red soles on her four-inch black stilettos.

"What is this about, Ogún? Why have you come here?"

"One of the descendants of the Lost Children has been discovered. A woman." Ogún hesitated, then plowed on. "It is said that she caused thunder to roll, unbidden."

Oshun's expression of polite confusion turned to shock. "What?" At Ogún's nod, her expertly arched brows furrowed deeper. "Thunder? That could only mean...:

Ogún's expression was grim as he finished her sentence. "That the child is a descendant of Changó's. Yes."

Shock gave way to anger. Oshun was silent, then asked, "Does she bring lightning as well? Where lightning goes, thunder follows." When Ogún dropped his eyes, Oshun's anger became rage. "How dare he? How dare they both?" She sprang from the couch, fists clenched. The Zen fountain on her desk splashed erratically, dampening the papers on her desk. Ogún watched her pace back and forth for a few minutes, muttering imprecations in Yoruba, her heels striking the floor hard enough to make deep indentations in the thick carpet. Finally she slowed, then stopped. She walked over to the wide window behind her desk and stared, unseeing, at the traffic below on Piedmont Road.

"Is this for certain?" she finally asked.

Ogún nodded. "It is assumed, as there are no other *orisha* to grant such powers."

"Do they know? Does my husband know that his powers rest in a human child?"

38

"I am not sure. But I am sure that Eshú
has informed Yemajá or Aganjú, at the very
least."

"And they will tell Changó." She fiddled
with the pin on her hip as she continued to stare
out the window. "And my sister?"

"Again, I do not know."

Oshun nodded. "Changó will confront Oyá;
I find it hard to believe that he knew. He would
have rent the heavens, if that were so. As for
Oyá," she turned and walked back toward Ogún.
"She may not be the most maternal of the *orisha*,
but she will have placed the child under
protection, even if it was not a child that she had
borne." Her hips swayed as she approached
Ogún. "I want to find this child."

Ogún could only stare as Oshun unzipped
her skirt at the side of her waist, allowing it to
fall to the ground. She wore matching gold lace
underwear that peeked through a black and gold
lace garter belt that held up the stockings. She
straddled him and leaned forward to nip at his
earlobe. He felt her warm breath caress the
sensitive skin of his ear. "Will you help me,
Ogún?"

Ogún buried his face in the valley of her
breasts as her hand unzipped the fly of his black

slacks and teased his massive erection from the front opening of his underwear. "You have only to ask," he mumbled as he freed an erect nipple from her bra and suckled.

***

The heavy drum and bass of the dance music pulsated throughout the club. Bodies jumped and gyrated to the beat in joyous abandon. Colorful strobe lights flashed to the rhythm, causing a freeze-frame effect that was, at times, reminiscent of a horror show.

"What are they doing?" Aganjú yelled over the music as he and Yemajá forced their way through the thick crowd. His human form was dressed in what Yemajá assured him was appropriate modern club wear. How humans wore these "skinny jeans" was beyond him; he'd never felt so constricted in all of his thousands of years of existence.

"Dancing," Yemajá yelled back over her shoulder. Her human form this evening had blue-streaked black hair and blue eyes set in golden-hued skin, over which she wore fashionable round glasses with a faint blue tint.

Aganjú shook his head. Humans called this dancing? And music? Whatever happened to the proper motions to the visceral sounds of the carimbo, gbedu, djembe, Batá? He gave an unheard sigh as they approached the source of the music. Women in tight, revealing clothing, high heels, elaborate hairstyles and heavy makeup posed themselves around the platform booth, which was emblazoned with a logo of a double-headed golden axe against a large Batá drum. They shot admiring stares at DJ Djembe himself as he worked the gold-rimmed double turntables atop the booth. One large, brown hand pressed one-half of his metallic red headphone cups against an ear as his head bopped to the beat; the other hand expertly slid the series of equalizers up and down to provide optimal music experience to the dancers below. An open red MacBook Pro computer showed the music in electronic form, the lines jumping and scrolling across the screen like a techno version of an EKG.

The DJ glanced over at the computer monitor and became aware of the two gods in human form nearby. His eyebrows shot up in surprise before he tapped some buttons on the computer and laid his headphones aside. He cupped one woman under the chin, tweaked the nipple of a second and caressed the bottom of a third as the small crowd of women parted to let him pass. He accepted a drink from the bartender as he passed the bar on his way to a narrow corridor that housed the restrooms. He passed long lines of people waiting to relieve themselves and went through a black-painted door, which led to a short flight of stairs.

Aganjú and Yemajá caught up with the DJ, which was one of Changó's favored human forms. He sat on a futon couch in the club owner's ramshackle office, his long legs stretched out and encased in white track suit bottoms with red racing stripes up the sides. A red T-shirt slicked across his developed chest.

"*Iya, Baba,*" Changó greeted with a toothy grin after a sip of his drink. "Surprised to see you here." His grin widened as he took in Aganjú's black skinny jeans and white T-shirt beneath a burnt orange vest embroidered with golden suns. "Nice threads, *Baba.*"

"I think he looks quite handsome," Yemajá said over Changó's chuckle at Aganjú's glare. "Anyway, we are not here to discuss fashion."

"I figured as much." He eyed his parents over the rim of his glass. "Whatever it is must be serious to get you to come here."

"It is." Yemajá removed her glasses and tucked them into the breast pocket of her oversized, floral-embroidered shirt. "Are you aware of the *omo sọnu olorun?*"

"The Lost Children? Of course. Glad I never had that problem." He raised his glass to take another sip of his drink, but lowered it at the exchanged glance between his parents. "What's going on?"

Yemajá took a deep breath. "Eshú and Babalúayé found a human woman who could cause thunder and lightning."

Changó stared at his mother. "Impossible."

Yemajá shook her head. "There is no reason for them to lie, especially given the potential consequences."

It was Changó's turn to shake his head, though more forcefully than his mother. "Impossible," he repeated.

"Why is it impossible, son?" Aganjú asked. "You do have a way with the ladies; three in particular."

Changó waved a hand in irritation. "Yet in all these millennia, I have only procreated with Oshun, who bore the Ibeji."

"That you know of."

"*Baba*, do you really think that something of that magnitude could be hidden from me? *Me*, Changó?"

"That depends on who is doing the hiding."

Changó mulled over that statement. He shook his head a third time, but in resignation instead. "Oba would never dare. Oshun would try, but she would give herself away. Oyá, definitely. But any child borne of them would be *orisha* as well, as the Ibeji are." He paused; the red-striped, white sneaker on his left foot beat a muffled staccato against the thinly carpeted floor. "You said this human woman could bring thunder and lightning? Unbidden?"

Yemajá nodded. "That is what Eshú reported. But apparently the woman is unaware of her powers; she did it once, by accident."

Changó fiddled with his glass as a memory crossed his mind. A human woman, decades ago. But surely... He drained the glass and the tattoo of a double-headed axe rippled on his biceps. "I would have to see this woman for myself. Then I will know for sure."

"Olodumare strictly forbid direct contact between *orisha* and the *omo sọnu olorun*," Aganjú reminded him.

Changó shrugged. He didn't care overmuch for rules that he didn't make himself; he had once been a popular human king, after all. "There's no harm in looking, *Baba*. Plus, she's not really my *omo sọnu olorun*, now is she? She's the alleged offspring of two of them, and human for all intents and purposes." He paused and regarded his parents. "I take it you are not the only ones aware of this...situation?"

Yemajá squirmed in her seat. "We are not aware of who knows, exactly," she admitted.

"I heard it from Eshú," Aganjú added.

"Which means that the rumor will have fallen on the ears of most, if not all, of the *orisha*. Eshú would derive great pleasure from stirring up controversy, bless his trickster heart." Changó sighed. "Which means Ogún will be rushing to tell Oshun, if he hasn't already." He rose, standing to his full human height of almost seven feet tall. "I have many enemies among the *orisha* and those who serve them, as you well know. Ah, well." He stretched, arms over his head and back arched. "I have not been in a true battle for decades. This might even be fun."

"Surely you don't mean to fight Ogún?" Yemajá was not pleased; Ogún was Changó's half-brother.

"Whether or not I prefer it, *Iya*, he will want to fight me. You know he never got over that Oyá business."

"Well, you did take his wife away from him, Changó," Aganjú admonished.

"You can't take someone if they are willing to go. Was it my fault that she preferred me? Oyá was too much woman for him, anyway. She and I are much better suited." He walked over and gave his mother a kiss on the cheek before embracing his father. "I must go."

Yemajá laid a hand on his arm. "Promise me you won't do anything rash, Changó."

"You know better than to ask that of me, *Iya*." Changó winked, grinned, and left the room.

THREE

I struggled to my feet, clutching my side as I stared at the immobile body of the soldier. I limped over to him, moving slowly in deference to my injuries as well as caution, in case he got up again. I noticed that no one had approached the street, though I saw the crowd streaming ahead at the main thoroughfare. No one else had even come to retrieve their car from the many parked on both sides of the street, though it was possible that some of the cars belonged to the inhabitants of the homes. Even then, no one came out of their houses to see what happened.

I stared down in horror. There was a large, gaping hole in the middle of his chest, and what once were his uniform buttons and insignia were now fused hunks of metal. Smoke wafted from the blackened edges of the wound; the soldier's face was frozen in an expression of pained surprise, his grey eyes staring up at nothing. I tried to wrap my mind around the fact that I did that, somehow; I killed a man. Even worse, I killed a soldier in the United States Military. I was a civilian Black woman: they'd throw me in Guantanamo Bay and let me rot for that.

The patter of running feet caught my attention. I looked up and Navasha was running toward me, her purple scarf flying behind her. Even through my haze of shock and pain, I thought that she moved pretty well for an elder.

She ran up to me and skidded to a stop; loose pebbles scattered beneath her sneakers. Her chest heaved as she looked me up and down. "Are you alright?" she gasped.

"I'm a bit banged up, but I'll live." My eyes slid back over to the dead cop. Navasha followed my gaze and her eyes widened. She grabbed my arm and dragged me back to my car. "We must go now."

"The doors are already unlocked." We both climbed in and I pulled off and drove in the direction of my apartment. I was grateful for the steering wheel; holding onto it hid the tremors in my hands.

"You can't go home," Navasha said as she turned to look out of the rear window. "Go to my house." She gave me directions and we pulled into the driveway of a two-story house painted white with deep purple trim. She ushered me into her home and locked the door behind me. "Sit," she urged as she led me down a short hallway and gestured for me to sit down in the living room. "I'll be right back."

I sat down on a comfortable beige couch scattered with decorative throw pillows in shades of purple and burgundy. A loveseat and chair in the same upholstery were all grouped around a low, round wooden table of a light-colored wood; probably pine. The table matched the honeyed hue of the hardwood floors, which was covered in the hall by a runner of purple flowers on a cream-colored background. The table rested upon a much larger version of the runner in the hall. Various colorful portraits of African folklore graced the walls; my attention was drawn to one in particular. I stood and got closer, intrigued by the figure in the picture. It was a woman--I assumed it was a woman--dressed in a dress made of golden-tinged fluttering strings of cloth. Her face was covered by a mask of the same material. She danced across the tops of some tombstones, around which grew fat, purple eggplants hanging on thick, green vines. The background of the card was a gorgeous purple only a shade or two lighter than the eggplants. Lightning flashed from a cloud in the sky, and the woman held one of the lightning bolts in her hand.

"That is Oyá," Navasha said as she re-entered the room. She placed a bowl of water, a bottle of hand soap, and a soft-sided red case with a large white cross on it: a first aid kit.

"The African storm goddess?"

"Yes. There are rumors that she is the *orisha* upon which the comic book character Storm was created." She unzipped the case to reveal packets of sterile gauze, bandages, medical tape, and other first-aid paraphernalia. She removed some gauze pads and a tube of antibiotic ointment. "Let's look at your injuries."

She cleaned the scrapes with soap and water, applied ointment, and covered them with gauze pads wrapped with a roll of gauze. She palpated my side where the police officer had kicked me, noting my wince of pain. "Your ribs are probably cracked," she said. "Nothing to do for that but bind them. Lift your shirt, please?" I complied and she removed a wide elastic bandage from the kit. She wound it tightly around my lower torso and fastened it with metal clasps. "That's going to hurt for a few days; just take something over the counter, like ibuprofen."

"How do you know all this?" I asked as I pulled my shirt back down. My side still hurt, but

I felt better with my wounds cleaned and bandaged.

"I was a nurse in my former life." She smiled, and took the bowl of blood-tinged water and the first aid kit back to wherever she got them. When she returned this time, she had a glass of water and a small orange-brown bottle of pills. "This should help with the pain, for now." She shook one tablet into my gauze-covered palm. "It's Vicodin, left over from a car accident last year."

I chased it down with water. "Thank you for all of your help, Navasha. I really appreciate it." I sat back in the chair and waited for the painkiller to kick in. "What were you doing on that street, anyway?"

"I knew you were in trouble."

I shot her a curious look. "How?"

"Oyá told me in a vision."

"Excuse me?"

"Oyá came to me while I was at the shop and told me that you were in danger. I already had a bad feeling about that soldier; he wore the beads of an Ogún initiate beneath his uniform jacket."

"Who?"

"Ogún, the *orisha* of metal and battle. He also controls the military, law enforcement, and anything to do with construction and transportation. In short, anything that involves metal; that includes swords, knives, guns, medical equipment, modern technology, et cetera."

I could only stare at her for some sign that she was joking, but she seemed to be quite serious. "Okay," I managed to say. "How do you know about this Ogún? And Oyá?"

"I have served Oyá for over twenty years." She held up her wrist to display a bracelet of brown beads with thin white stripes, alternated with burgundy and purple beads. "Oyá and Ogún were once married, until Oyá ran off with Changó, his half-brother."

"Huh?" I started to shake my head, but stopped when the headache returned. "This all sounds like some sort of sordid adult soap opera."

"The *orisha* can be messy at times," Navasha admitted.

"What is an *orisha*?"

"The *orisha* are the African gods," Navasha explained. "A significant number come from the Yoruba tradition, but there are gods and goddesses from other traditions as well. There is even an overlap of *orisha* for those who practice Santería and Lukúmi, which are popular religions in other places where slaves were brought from Africa, like Cuba and Puerto Rico."

"Santería...that's like voodoo, right?"

"There are similarities between Santería and *vodu*, yes."

"Do they kill chickens too? And drink their blood?"

Navasha rolled her eyes. "Animal sacrifice is an accepted practice within both religions. As for the drinking of blood, *vodunsi* are not vampires."

"So wait a minute." I held up a hand as I tried to process this information. "You're telling me that you...serve an African goddess."

"Yes."

"And this has what to do with me? You said that Oyá told you I was in danger." Saying it out loud sounded just as crazy as it felt.

Navasha bit her bottom lip; it was obvious that she was deciding how much to say. "Some years ago, during one of my meditations, Oyá spoke to me and told me that there was a child of her lineage that needed protection. I was assigned to give you human protection to the best of my ability, while providing a conduit for her divine protection."

"So you're saying that I'm a descendant of an African storm goddess?" At Navasha's nod, I laughed. "What are you smoking? I'd like to try some of it."

"No drugs were ingested during the relay of this information," Navasha joked.

My laughter died. "You're serious," I said after a lengthy pause.

"Very much so."

"Okay." I rubbed my palms across my face; a sudden wave of exhaustion washed over me. "Let's say, for the sake of argument, that you're right about all this. How do you know for sure it's me? Maybe your Oyá mixed up your vision, or something."

Navasha's half-smile was disconcerting. She cocked her head to the side. "Have you had anything odd happen to you over the past month or so?"

"Other than somehow shooting lightning out of my hand and killing a soldier?"

Navasha chuckled. "Other than that, yes."

I thought back to that strange hiking trip. "When I went hiking a few weeks ago, I fell down a hill and twisted my ankle. I also hit my head.

54

These two men came out of the woods, out of nowhere. I mean, one minute I was by myself in the woods and the next these two appeared; but not together. One asked me for some candy and a smoke, and the other just healed my ankle."

Navasha sat forward with interest "Two men? What did they look like?"

"The first had on a red and black jacket, black pants and shoes. He's the one that asked me for candy. The other wore brown, and limped. He walked with a cane, and had chicken pox scars on the backs of his hands."

"You were visited by Eshú, the messenger *orisha* of the crossroads, and Babalúayé, one of the *orisha* of healing." She sat back with a smug look on her face.

"Okay..."

"You are under the protection of the *orisha*. They don't come to just anyone's aid."

"Fine. I'm under divine protection, or whatever." I waved off the statement in irritation. "But how did I get it? How did I become part of Oyá's goddess lineage, or legacy, or what have you? I'm Episcopalian."

"Is it safe to assume that you've never heard of the *omo sonu olorun*?"

"The who?" I shook my head. "Uh, yeah, it's safe to assume that."

Navasha's lips twitched in amusement. "Loosely translated from Yoruba, *omo ṣọnu olorun* means 'Lost Children of the Gods'. Once upon a time, as the story goes, the *orisha* had intimate relationships with humans, after the humans were created. Some of these unions resulted in half-human offspring of the *orisha*. Needless to say, some were not pleased at the presence of these offspring, thinking that they would upset the *orisha* balance of power, etc. So Olodumare the Supreme Creator, in her godhead of Olorun the Wise, decreed that the *omo ṣọnu olorun* be sent to earth to live as human, and the *orisha* were to have no further contact with them."

"I think I would have known if I'd had sex with a god." Given my current drought, I would have remembered any sex, period, but Navasha didn't need to know all that.

"I doubt that you did. You are not one of the Lost Children." She hesitated, then asked, "How are your parents?"

"My parents?" I tensed; that was not a topic I liked to discuss. "They're okay. Why?"

"Are they in good health?"

I wasn't sure how to answer that. "They're okay," I repeated.

"Mmm."

We sat in silence. The pain in my body receded as the painkiller took effect. My eyes drooped and I drifted off to sleep.

Then she came.

***

Dragonfly Venture Capitalists was one of the lesser known, yet well respected VC firms in the Bay Area. It had a reputation for funding projects that were true game changers, and not just rehashes of technology that already existed. Some of the companies it had backed went on to make millions of dollars; two went public and made billions. Still, Dragonfly VC only took on small projects, preferably by entrepreneurs and other small business owners; conglomerates need not apply.

This day, the founder and CEO of Dragonfly VC was in a troubled state of mind. Oyá stared out one of the windows of her large corner office at the blue-green waters of the San Francisco Bay. The chatter she'd been getting from the other *orisha* was disturbing. A descendant of the *omo sọnu olorun* who could call thunder and lightning just by thinking? The possibilities of this phenomenon certainly had the others in a state of gossipy concern. After all, when the Lost Children were banished to earth and forbade contact with the *orisha*, they all thought that was the end of the *orisha*/human dalliances.

Oyá sighed. That was the *orisha* for you: not that great on long-term consequences. Her fellow gods and goddesses did seem to be more checkers than chess. While such short-term thinking usually worked to their advantage this time it would come back to, as the humans liked to say, bite them all in the ass. Apparently, her personal short-sightedness was no exception.

She thought back to that gorgeous human, so many years ago. His lithe, muscular body, the gleam of his dark brown skin, his knack for engaging conversation, his respect with just the slightest tinge of fear...it was more than she was able to resist and she enjoyed their talks and acts of congress. Then he became too attached, and she had to leave him alone; surely he understood that *orisha* and humans were only meant to be together for a season--in fact, they weren't supposed to be together at all. Still, the *orisha* were no strangers to temptation, and Oyá was no different. She hated what became of that human consort, but it was necessary. To assuage her guilt, she placed protection around him that would be in place until his dying day. She also knew that he had married a human and that they had children--Oyá just never figured that their children would be anything out of the ordinary. How wrong she was; and if she was wrong, then what of the other descendants of the Lost Children? Were there others that had dormant powers that were soon to be brought to light? Or had they already manifested, yet were hidden for good reason?

Oyá paced around her office, the morning sunlight brightening the purple linen wallpaper embossed with faint gold whorls that, upon closer inspection, resembled hurricanes. Yet another problem presented itself within this storm--no pun intended--that was brewing among the *orisha*. According to a private word from Yeguá, the *orisha* of death, the human woman was said to be able to call thunder *and* lightning. Thunder was solely Changó's domain. Which mean that he, too, had consorted with a human and somehow, that human procreated with Oyá's human, and they produced this child.

Oyá shook her head, the amethyst earrings in her ears catching the light and reflecting aubergine glory. Impossible as it seemed, there was no other possible explanation for it, outside of Changó dallying with the human woman herself. But even Changó would not be that bold as to blatantly flout the rules that Olodumare, as Olorun, decreed. Speaking of Changó...Oyá was surprised that he had not tried to contact her at this time, if for no other reason than to demand an explanation. Unless he had no knowledge of the woman, which Oyá doubted; Changó had a very reliable network that kept him apprised of anything major going on among the *orisha*, and Eshú was quick to spread news, good or ill.

Oyá retrieved her purse from her desk and headed out. She needed to be outside, where she could think better. She told her assistant to call her on her cell phone if anything important happened and left the tall office building--which she owned, and leased out the other floors--to step into the bright sunshine. Her high heels clicked as she strolled through Embarcadero Square, pausing to look at the wares for sale by the independent artisans that gathered daily. In addition to storms, Oyá also ruled the marketplace and commerce, so anywhere that things were sold--whether online, or in a brick-and-mortar establishment, or in the open like these vendors--caught her interest. Farmers' markets were a particular favorite.

A light breeze caressed her face as she continued her journey past the firehouse near Pier 22. Two fire trucks were parked in the large driveway; firemen wearing simple navy blue uniform pants and T-shirts with the San Francisco Fire Department logo emblazoned over their left breasts. One of the firemen whistled at Oyá as she passed. She turned to look at him and got a wink in return. Oyá smiled and slowed. The fireman walked over to her, drying his hands on a damp rag.

"Fancy meeting you here," Changó greeted with a grin.

"I needed to clear my head. Surely you've heard of the rumors?"

"About the *omo sonu olorun* ? Of course. *Baba* and *Iya* told me."

"Of course." Oyá shouldn't have been surprised; Yemajá doted on Changó, and Aganjú went along with most of what Yemajá wanted; he was the most malleable of Yemajá's husbands.

Changó's eyes traveled over Oyá's curves beneath the tailored burgundy pantsuit. "You look good."

Oyá patted the crown of braids atop her head. "Thank you." She eyed Changó's broad shoulders beneath the T-shirt with appreciation. "I always liked you in your fireman form."

"More like you like me in the fireman's uniform."

"I like you even better without it."

Changó's grin was salacious. "See, now why are you starting something you can't finish? You know I'm on duty."

"That's never stopped us before."

Changó's eyes lit up in memory. "Yes, right on the back of Ladder 15, with my co-workers none the wiser." He looked back to where the truck in question was parked in its bay. "We could give it another go."

"Not right now," Oyá said as she ignored his wolfish grin. "We have more pressing matters to tend to."

Changó shrugged and tucked the rag in his pocket. "I will visit the human and see what there is to see. If she is indeed my lineage."

"Yes, about that." Oyá chose her words carefully. Her husband had a bit of a temper, though not as bad as that of his brother Ogún. "Changó, is it possible that one of your humans, and one of my humans, mated and had a child?"

Changó thought about it, his full lower lip poked out in concentration. "I suppose it is possible," he conceded. "If this is true, did you know that there was a human of my lineage involved?"

"I didn't even know that there was a human of *my* lineage involved, much less yours." Oyá looked at Changó; in her human form, she was six feet tall in her bare feet. In her high heels, she was able to look Changó in the eye since this particular human form of his was six foot three. "Did you not keep apprised of your humans?"

"Not really," Changó confessed. "I enjoyed my time with them but when it ended, I just went on about my business."

"How could you leave them like that, Changó? Humans are not as strong as we *orisha*; interaction with us could have devastating consequences." As she knew all too well.

Changó shrugged. "I cannot go back and change things. If there is recompense to be made, it must be done going forward." He eyed Oyá. "You did not know of this woman's existence?"

"No." Oyá shook her head. "I heard about it from one of my servants, while she communicated with me in meditation. Later, the rumors among the *orisha* were brought to my attention."

"Eshú?"

"No."

Changó waited for Oyá to elaborate further, but she remained silent. "Have you seen this human?"

"Not yet. I have her under protection, but it may not be enough. I will need to make myself known to her soon. She will need to learn how to harness her powers, and my servants can only do but so much." She looked at Changó. "Are you going to see her?"

Changó nodded. "I must. While I do not doubt the words and observations of Babalúayé, I need to determine this lineage for myself."

"I understand. And if Babalúayé is indeed telling the truth?"

"I will handle that when the time comes." He paused and said, "You know that Oshun is going to find out about all this, if she has not already."

"I know." Oyá gnawed at her berry-painted lips. "But Oshun is, as the humans say, a lover, not a fighter. She may grow angry, but her ire will be short-lived and she will move onto other things."

"What about Ogún?"

"What about him?"

"He is loyal to your sister."

"And?" Oyá laughed at Changó's look of concern. "Do not be alarmed. Ogún loves to fight, but this is not his battle."

"Do not underestimate him, Oyá. He does not see clearly where Oshun is concerned. And do not forget that he was one of the *orisha* in support of the Lost Children to be banished to Earth."

Oyá waved a manicured hand in dismissal. "Are you implying that Oshun will ask Ogún to harm the woman?"

"It wouldn't surprise me. The human woman's abilities are a reminder that we are together, and that I left Oshun for you. She will not take that lightly."

"Oshun wouldn't dare."

Changó shook his head. Oyá was a supreme warrior and leader; perhaps too good. Her confidence--and arrogance--was such that she would not expect anyone to overtly challenge her, which was why Oshun bore watching. The *orisha* employed subtle skills that made her as

formidable as her sister. However, Changó knew
not to waste his time trying to convince Oyá of
this. "Just be mindful that attack can come when
you least expect it." The fire alarm blared;
Changó looked back over his shoulder at the
other firemen, who had dropped their cleaning
items and were running into the firehouse to
change into their gear. "I must go." He ran a
finger down Oyá's cheek.

Oyá closed her eyes in pleasure. "Make
sure you stop by later."

"I wouldn't miss it." The fire truck roared
up beside him and he jumped aboard the side
before grabbing the fire coat that one of the
other firemen handed to him. He gave a jaunty
wave as the fire truck barreled down the
Embarcadero.

Oyá chose not to return to the office.
Instead, she flashed herself to the San Francisco
National Cemetery, in the Presidio. She strolled
along the paved paths and nodded to the spirits
of deceased humans that appeared before her.
Most had been soldiers in wars fought long ago;
all seemed to be content in the afterlife as they
floated past. Oyá stopped here and there,
neatening the flowers and other trinkets laid
before the granite headstones, removing dead

flowers, flicking dust from the stones so that they glowed a cool, slightly sparkly gray-white in the sunlight. She nodded at Yeguá, whose airy pink robes floated around her as she escorted a soul from a freshly dug grave to the afterlife. She ended up at a bench that had recently been vacated by some tourists and closed her eyes, enjoying the feel of the sun on her face and the slight breeze off nearby Baker Beach.

She needed to visit this human woman who was of her lineage. Her devoted servant Navasha had kept in contact with the woman for years, and Oyá was able to use that connection to feel when the woman was in danger and dispatch Navasha to help. Oyá had shied away from contacting the woman directly because she was not ready; unfortunately, events had escalated to the point where Oyá needed to make contact, whether the woman was ready or not. But if she was indeed of Oyá's lineage, she would have the fortitude to deal with speaking with the powerful *orisha*.

Oyá closed her eyes and sent her essence wide, across the country to the state of Georgia. In a city called Atlanta, she felt Navasha's spirit, and then the presence of another--the woman, her spiritual progeny. The woman's spirit was calm and measured--she was asleep, and deeply. Oyá nodded to herself in approval; it was easiest to visit humans in a dream state, when their normal barriers were relaxed.

***

I stood in the eye of a hurricane while the winds whipped around me. Strangely, I was not harmed. In fact, the wind felt good against my skin as my purple robes fluttered and molded to my body. Thunder rolled and lightning flashed past my head, but I didn't flinch.

She walked atop the winds toward me, the rags of her skirt showing toned brown legs that ended in bare feet. A machete was in one hand; a black whip made of some kind of hair in the other. Her upper torso was encased in purple beads draped across high, small breasts. Thick, dark dreadlocks cascaded across her bare shoulders and down her back. A mask made of palm fronds covered her face. She stepped into the eye of the storm and stopped a respectful distance from me. "Do you know who I am, daughter?" she asked. The palm fronds fluttered with each word she spoke.

"You are Oyá, ruler of storms and lightning, goddess of change and ancestors." I looked around at the winds and clouds spinning

in a lazy, counterclockwise circle. "Why am I here?"

"You are here because it is time for you to know who you really are."

"Who am I?"

She smiled, her full lips parting to display even, white teeth. She stepped close enough to kiss me on the forehead. Her locks smelled like a heavenly blend of no incense I'd ever encountered. At the same time, she pressed a hand against my forearm. A brief flare of pain, then nothing.

Oyá stepped away. "You are mine."

I woke up, disoriented, and looked around the room with bleary eyes. It took me a minute to remember where I was: Navasha's house. Then I remembered the events that led me here, and Navasha's revelations.

I looked over at the picture of the woman on the wall, wearing the palm frond mask, dancing on tombstones. Oyá. My dream returned to me and I was aware of an ache in my arm. Probably a by-product of the attack by the soldier, when I was knocked to the ground. I went to rub the offended area and froze in disbelief. On my forearm, where the skin was bare before, was now a dark mark shaped like a hurricane.

***

The warm rush of air from the tunnel signaled to Ogún that the train was coming. Seconds later, the silver subway train barreled into the station. The doors chimed open and passengers spilled out the double doors in each car. Ogún boarded right before the doors closed. He looked around for a seat, but there were none to be had; he settled for a vinyl-covered hand strap on the horizontal pole above his head.

Ogún was staring blankly at the large advertisement for a new type of toothpaste when he felt a surge of energy from his left side. He glanced sideways and noticed the pretty woman in a purple dress and matching head wrap holding on to the adjacent hand strap with one hand. Her other hand held a folded newspaper. He turned his attention back to the advertisement. "Oyá."

"Ogún." Oyá peered at her former husband over her burgundy tortoise shell-patterned glasses. "Fancy meeting you here."

"I could say the same. Subways aren't your usual style."

"It's good to try something different every now and again. Flashing here and there can grow boring." She looked down at the newspaper in her hand, as if she were just another indifferent commuter. "The question is, why are you here? You don't often come to the human realm."

"You are not the only one who has business here."

Oyá looked back up at Ogún. "I never said I was. But your love of solitude is well known, as is your overall disdain for humans. So why would you come here?"

Ogún tapped the metal buckle of his belt with a large finger. "I had other business to attend to in this realm."

Oyá frowned. Ogún was not a subtle man, and his mannerisms often gave a clue to his state of mind. Tapping his finger on a piece of metal was a sure sign of nervousness. "What have you been doing, Ogún?"

"What?" The tapping increased as discomfort passed across his face.

Oyá shifted to her right, pressing her body closer. "Answer me, Ogún."

Ogún glared at the other *orisha*. "I no longer answer to you, Oyá."

"On that, we agree." She looked closely at him. "But to whom do you answer, now?"

"No one! I am my own man."

Oyá cocked her head, the brown eyes behind the lenses deepening with concern. "Have you been in contact with my sister? Does Oshun have you doing her bidding, still?"

Ogún glared at her. "This is none of your concern, Oyá."

"About that." She shifted her weight as the train pulled into the next station. "A descendant of my lineage was attacked out of the blue by a military soldier a short time ago. You wouldn't happen to know anything about that, would you?"

"The affairs of humans do not concern me," Ogún sneered.

"I agree. Except this soldier targeted my descendant only. He waited until she had left a shop and was on her way home. Luckily, one of my servants got to her in time."

"She was fortunate indeed."

"Yes." She was jostled as some commuters in the seats behind her got up to exit the train at the upcoming station. "Was the police officer under your control, Ogún?" At Ogún's silence, the breeze from the open car doors blew into the car stronger, scattering the odd paper cup that someone had left on the floor. It rattled up and down the aisles while commuters looked around in confusion and held tighter to poles and hand straps. "Answer me!"

Ogún braced his body against the strong breeze. "It does not matter. The human woman, your descendant, finished what I started."

Oyá sucked her teeth. "You should know better than to attack my descendants; my power flows through them. But why was she attacked in the first place? Was she doing something to cause harm?"

"That depends on your definition of harm."

"Who asked you to harm the woman? The woman of my lineage?"

Ogún snorted in defiance to cover up a sudden flash of guilt. "What do you care? It is clear that you have more pressing matters on your mind, like being with Changó." Beads of sweat popped out on his forehead, another sure sign of nervousness.

"Are you still dwelling on that?" Oyá shook her head with a frown. "You keep evading my questions. What have you done, Ogún?"

"What?" The tapping increased as discomfort passed across his face.

Oyá stepped even closer, crowding her tall, lithe frame into Ogún's personal space. Her voice dropped to a growl of warning. "Answer me, Ogún."

"It does not matter. Oshun will have her way."

Comprehension dawned on Oyá's face. "Oshun asked you to harm the woman? The woman of my lineage?" Ogún's suddenly downcast eyes told Oyá everything she needed to know. She let loose with a blood-curdling battle cry that shook the tempered glass windows of the subway and had the remaining commuters diving for cover among cries and screams of fear and panic. There was a flash of light, then Oyá disappeared.

***

Oyá flashed into the rear of a dance studio. The warm room was filled with leotarded bodies lined up in five precise rows, male and female, facing the dance instructor at the front of the room. The mirrored wall behind the instructor reflected her curvaceous shape, clad in a yellow, full-length leotard. The tank straps displayed her rounded brown shoulders and toned arms. Her muscular legs peeked through the sheer dance skirt in a peacock feather print that swirled with each movement. Another woman, clad in a dark blue leotard and pale blue leg warmers, crouched to the side in front of a stereo system.

The instructor turned to face the mirror, giving her a full view of her class. "Let's do that combination again. And give me some feeling this time! Five...six...five, six, seven, eight!"

The dark-clad woman pressed a button on the stereo and a sensual bass line wafted out from the speakers. The instructor led the class in a series of leaps, kicks, and spins that segued into hip-shaking steps and artistic rolls on the floor. The class ended with their hands in the air, posing. The instructor turned and faced the class. Her eyes drifted toward the back and spotted Oyá. Only the slight twitch beneath an eye gave any indication that she paid attention to the *orisha*'s presence. "That was great, guys! Okay, take five."

The class broke formation and rushed to the gym bags and water bottles that were littered around the periphery of the studio. As the students and the assistant instructor filed out of the room, the instructor strode toward the back of the room. "Hello, sister," the woman said as she approached Oyá.

Oyá tipped her head in greeting. "Oshun."

Oshun wiped her forearm across her sweaty forehead. "What brings you here? Slumming?"

"Hardly." Oyá looked around the large studio, taking in the golden tone of the wooden floors and the deep yellow walls that glowed in the light that flowed from the large windows that were cracked to let in air. "I saw Ogún today."

"Really? And he managed not to kill you? He must be mellowing as the years pass."

Oyá ignored the barb. "He let an interesting tidbit slip: something about a job he did for you."

"For me?" Oshun flicked her long, gold-streaked brown braid over her shoulder in an effort to stall for time. How did Oyá find out? "I have no idea what you're talking about."

"Really? Because Ogún made it sound like he attacked a human of my lineage, on your orders. And we both know that Ogún is not given to flights of fancy."

Oshun shrugged in an effort to cover up her panic. Oyá was not to be trifled with and sister or no sister, the storm goddess was formidable in her wrath. "Ogún must have taken something I said out of context."

Oyá gave her younger sister a measured look. "Ogún is not one to act on a misconstrual. He prefers plain talk to innuendo or suggestion."

Oshun sucked her teeth in irritation. "Then you need to take that up with him." She peeked at the smartwatch on her wrist, then looked back up at Oyá. "Are we done here? I have to get back to my class."

Oyá stared at her sister. A light breeze that wafted through the open windows grew stronger; the door to the studio slammed shut. Oshun's eyes widened, then narrowed. "I think you need to leave, Oyá."

In response, Oyá merely caused the breeze to increase; the mirrored wall shimmered and the stereo blew back against the wall and was pinned there.

Oshun stood firm against the strong winds, her dance skirt fluttering enough for the ties to loosen around her waist. She waved a manicured hand and a stream of water from a nearby open bottle flew out and wafted toward Oshun. She waved her hand again and the water formed a lasso, which she threw at her sister.

STORMBRINGER

Oyá raised a hand and whipped the watery lasso into a mini-hurricane. The counterclockwise rotation of the miniature storm sucked up random debris and dust that had tracked into and across the room over the course of the class.

Oshun glowered and pulled even more water out of the bottle, this time expanding it to form a thin wall of water. She heaved the liquid wall at Oyá, who used the force of wind to blow the wall back at Oshun. The river goddess shrieked as the water broke across her body, soaking her to the skin. "How dare you," she yelled as she wrung water out of her long braid.

Oyá flexed a hand; lightning pooled in her palm. She was satisfied to see Oshun's eyes widen in fear of being electrocuted. "Let this be a warning to you, sister: no harm is to come to anyone else of my lineage, by your thought, word, or deed, or else you will suffer the full brunt of my ire."

Oshun merely glared at Oyá as she manipulated the puddle of water on the floor and sent it out a window in a steady stream.

"Have a care, sister. Cross me at your peril." Satisfied that her sister was momentarily cowed, Oyá flashed out of the studio.

STORMBRINGER

****FOUR****

Over the next couple of weeks, I scoured the online newspapers for any mention of the dead soldier, but nothing showed up. Nothing. Which was odd, since a soldier's death almost always made headlines in some way. When I asked Navasha about it, she looked worried, but brushed it off. "I'll explain later," she said and hurried off to help a customer.

It was another month and a half before I had healed enough to resume my aikido. I walked out of my first practice since my hiking incident sweaty and sore, but feeling good. Physically, that is. Emotionally and mentally, I was not dealing well with the whole being-marked-by-an-*orisha* thing. Which was to say: I avoided thinking about it. I covered up the mark with an adhesive bandage, and wore long sleeves whenever possible. Being that we were having an Indian summer in Atlanta, this presented a bit of a challenge.

Since that crazy day I'd been on the Internet, looking up information about Oyá, to supplement Navasha's lessons and a book she gave me to read about the African *orisha*. Oyá was mainly known for ruling lightning and storms, and cemeteries (but not the dead or

80

death, per se; another, lesser-known *orisha* had
that honor). She was actually best known in
Africa for ruling the marketplace and commerce.
I thought back to all of my previous jobs, since
high school; they'd all been some sort of sales
position, and I'd always done very well at them.
Even now, working in the development office for
a museum. "Development" was just a nonprofit
code word for sales: getting people to part with
their money, or gifts in kind like permanent
installments or loan pieces.

I thought back to that day in the park
when I twisted my ankle; right after the injury,
the sky suddenly darkened and then there was
thunder. Then there was the incident with the
cop and the lightning shooting out of my hand.
Navasha said that it happened because Oyá was
channeling her powers through me: that was part
of her protection. "But you can't just go around
shooting lightning at people," Navasha warned.
"This isn't a Marvel Comics film."

For all of my research, I still couldn't
figure out why I was one of Oyá's chosen. What
made me so special? Navasha didn't have an
answer, either--or rather, she refused to speak at
length on the matter. She still gave me the

"You're not ready to know" spiel, and it was
getting tiresome.

During the course of my research, I
noticed two other *orisha* names that kept coming
up in conjunction with Oyá. Navasha had
mentioned them in passing: Changó and Ogún.
Changó, according to legend, was Oyá's second
husband (or lover, depending on the source).
Ogún, it seems, was her first husband, and she
left him for Changó. Ogún then took up with
Oshun, Oyá's sister and Changó's second wife
(Oyá was his third). Messy, indeed. But before
she broke camp to be with Changó, Oyá and
Ogún were actually a rather formidable couple.
They fought side by side in battle; it was Ogún
who forged the twin machetes that were Oyá's
preferred weapons. Changó, however, proved to
be more of a soul-level match for the storm
goddess.

I remembered an old adage: where
lightning appears, thunder follows. Again, I
thought back to that day I injured myself hiking.
I heard thunder first, but that doesn't mean the
lightning wasn't there. I was too distracted by
pain to look for it, only noticing the sudden storm
clouds. Which brought me to yet another strange
thought: if I caused lightning, then was I able to

cause thunder too? And if so, then did this mean I somehow had Changó's powers, since he was the only *orisha* I could find that ruled thunder? Yet another question to ask Navasha, and yet another question which she'd probably blow off under the "need to know" excuse--the excuse being that I didn't need to know, yet. I had to admit to myself that I wouldn't even know what to do with that information; it was hard enough wrapping my mind around the Oyá connection. If I was found to be a descendant of yet another *orisha*, my head would probably explode.

***

No matter how many times I visited Pine Breezes Assisted Living Facility, I would never get used to the overpowering scent of fake oranges, or the underlying odor of decay, death, and depression. The facility had won awards for the rehabilitation and recovery of some of its patients. Unfortunately for me, the hand of healing hadn't quite made it to my father, and probably never would.

"Good morning, Violet," greeted Hazel, one of the old-school nurses in the place. Hazel had been at Pine Breezes since it opened over thirty years ago, and would probably be buried there.

"Morning, Miss Hazel."

Hazel clucked her tongue in admonishment. "How many times do I have to tell you that it's just 'Hazel'?"

"And how many times do I have to tell you that it was the way I was brought up? It's a sign of respect."

Hazel smiled and patted her silver-white hair, which was pulled back in its usual no-nonsense bun at the nape of her neck. "You don't see too much respect from the young ones these days."

"I'm a seventies child, so I'm not claiming this new generation." I abandoned the light-hearted banter. "Any change?"

Hazel's smile dimmed. "Not really, Violet. Your father is still...well...," She sighed. "Although he's been very agitated lately, especially at night. Seeing you would do him some good."

I nodded and gave a close-lipped smile that didn't reach my eyes. Despite her optimism, I knew that my father would never be the jovial, larger-than-life man I vaguely remembered as child. And he would never leave this place.

I entered his room, which was at its normal temperature of "tropical". Dad was seated in the recliner chair in front of a window, hunched over a sketch pad. Stray beams of sunlight caressed the crown of his head in a makeshift halo that bounced off the brown skin peeking through his thinning, close-cropped salt-and-pepper hair. His lips were pursed in concentration as he pushed the charcoal pencil in furious swathes across the page.

"Hi, Dad."

Charles Davidson grunted but remained focused on his drawing.

"Whatcha working on?" I moved closer to see; the drawing seemed to be a series of hurricanes, their counterclockwise spirals surrounding vacant eyes in the center. "Dad?"

"I have to make her a gift for when she visits," he mumbled. "I have to make offering so that she will listen to me and protect me."

Nerves jangled in my midsection. "Who, Dad?"

"The Mother of Nine."

I wasn't sure who the Mother of Nine was, though the hurricanes gave me an idea. I looked around the claustrophobic room; Dad had gone through a phase where he was really into rainbows. The walls were plastered with drawings of rainbows and pictures of them cut out of magazines. The mini-refrigerator I convinced the center to let him have (he loved drinking Yoo Hoos and I made sure he had a supply) had rainbow-shaped magnets affixed to its door. I'd hung a crystal teardrop from the curtain rod over his window, and the sunlight refracted into rainbows that danced across the room.

"The Mother of Nine is mighty fine," he sang off-key as he continued to draw.

"I brought you some stuff, Dad." I placed the plastic bags on his bed. "The nurses said you needed new pajamas, so I got you some. And a book on rainbows."

"Storms."

"What?"

Dad finally looked up from his drawing. For the first time in a long time, clarity lived in his deep brown eyes. "Storms are coming, Baby Girl. Be ready. She'll protect you, though."

I swallowed a sudden rush of tears. Dad hadn't called me Baby Girl since he came to this facility over five years ago. Sometimes I wondered if he even remembered who I was.

"Violet." Dad fixed me with a beseeching look.

My heart flipped at the sound of my name from his lips. "Yes, Dad?"

"You see her, right? You see Oyá?"

I sank down onto the edge of his full-sized bed in shock.

"You see her, right? Because she said she'd come to you when the storms started. She promised."

The childlike earnestness in his voice was almost too much. "I see her, Dad," I managed to choke out before I rushed into his bathroom. Hot tears streaked down my face as I sobbed into my hands. The events of the past month, my father's sudden bout of clarity, which got me to wondering about my mother...it was way too much for my fragile emotional state.

I got myself together and exited the bathroom. Dad had not moved from his spot by the window. I sat back down on the bed. "Dad? How do you, um, know Oyá?"

"Been with Oyá for years." Dad had gone back to work on his drawing.

I waited for him to say more, but the only sounds in the room were of our respective breathing and his pencil gliding across the paper. "But how did you meet her?"

"Never saw a woman that fine in all my born years. Tall, dark, and smooth, like a bottle of blackstrap molasses. Yep," he sighed as he raised his head and stared out the window, lost in memory. "Never seen a woman like that. Men who'd have women at the snap of a finger steered clear of her like she was a queen, like they were afraid of being shot down. Then she saw me." He chuckled, a rusty sound like he didn't do it often. "I was kind of a looker in my younger days, if I do say so myself, but nothing special."

I'd seen old pictures of him, when he was a young man. He was indeed good-looking but, like he said, there was nothing out of the ordinary about his handsomeness.

"Why she picked me, I had no idea, but I wasn't about to look a gift horse in the mouth. I would've been a new kind of fool if I did." He continued to stare out the window, this time looking at the sky. "Surprised me when we went back to the room she had in a nice hotel. I'd never seen a Negro so comfortable in such nice surroundings. That room fit her like she was born to luxury. And the sheets on that bed were so smooth..." His voice trailed off into silence. Before I could prompt him (and pray that he didn't go into further detail about That Night), he continued. "Next morning, she was gone. Luggage, clothes...like she was never there. All that was left behind was a ring." His gaze trailed down to where the gold ring with the large, oval-shaped amethyst and weird markings around the band rested on his right hand, which I'd never seen him without--not even when he was in the hospital to have his appendix removed when I was ten. "And this mark."

I watched him touch the back of his left shoulder at that last remark. I knew that beneath his shirt, visible even in the sleeveless undershirts that he favored, was a large, borderline oval-shaped mark that was several shades darker than his medium-brown skin. I unconsciously touched the area on my arm where my matching mark rested beneath my sleeve.

Before I could comment further, there was a brisk knock on the door. A tall man entered in a white lab coat over his pressed khaki slacks and a white dress shirt. His tie was a bright turquoise blue scattered with yellow flecks. Surprise flashed across his face at my presence, though he quickly schooled his face into a more neutral expression. "I'm sorry, Mr. Davidson," the man apologized, looking at me. "I didn't know you had a visitor."

"It's Erinle!" Dad became positively perky at the sight of the doctor.

The doctor looked even more startled at the mention of his name; he shot Dad a look of warning. I frowned; I understood that some doctors were sticklers for being addressed by their titles; this doctor may have been one of those. I looked at his ID badge, which had his picture and the name "E. Inle, N.D." in bold, black letters. "I'm Violet Davidson, Dr. Inle," I said as I held out my hand. "I'm his daughter."

Dr. Inle shook my hand and scrutinized me with golden brown eyes that were only enhanced by the gold rim-framed glasses he wore. "Nice to meet you."

"What kind of doctor are you? I've met everyone on my dad's care team, but I don't remember you."

"I'm a new hire," Dr. Inle explained. "I'm here to assess the needs of our longer-term residents, to see if some of their health issues can be alleviated by a more holistic approach."

I looked at his ID badge again. "N.D.; what kind of doctor is that?"

"I am a naturopathic doctor. I went to medical school, but our focus included botanical and homeopathic medicine."

I raised an eyebrow. "So you're going to try and heal my father with herbs and berries?"

"If I can. At the very least, I can ease some of his periods of agitation."

"Huh." That would be helpful; sometimes Dad got so keyed up that he was unable to sleep.

"Mr. Davidson, I have your sleeping drink." He removed a small glassine packet of a greenish powder from the pocket of his lab coat. To me he explained, "We are trying him on an herbal concoction to stimulate rest. It contains chamomile, melatonin, and St, John's wort, among other things."

I watched as Dr. Inle poured a glass of water from the pitcher on Dad's nightstand and added the powder to it. The powder seemed to dissolve into the water without stirring. He handed the greenish liquid to Dad, who drank it down without protest. "That's good," he announced after a large belch.

Dr. Inle chuckled. "He really seems to like the taste; I wish I could say the same of all my patients."

"So that drink mix is going to make him fall asleep?"

"He'll be calmer soon; in some patients they are merely quieter but the herbal mix seems to make Mr. Davidson sleepy instead."

"And that herbal mix isn't addictive, or will give him adverse side effects?"

Dr. Inle shook his head as he tucked the empty plastic envelope back into his pocket. "No. The individual components are readily available at any vitamin store, farmers' market, or health food store. I made sure that they didn't interfere with any other medications he may have taken. But your father has no significant physical illness, so I was more than comfortable in giving it to him. And he has responded well; the night shift nurses say that he sleeps more soundly than ever, and doesn't talk in his sleep anymore."

Dad's narcoleptic chatter was a cause of concern and irritation among his care team. "Well, if it works and he isn't harmed, then I'm all for it." I checked my watch; I had to meet Navasha for another learning session. "I have to go. It was nice meeting you, Dr. Inle."

"Likewise. Let me walk you out."

Dr. Inle escorted me to the lobby, where I waved goodbye to Miss Hazel and left for my appointment with Navasha.

***

Erinle, also known as Inle, watched until Violet Davidson had completely left the grounds before retracing his steps back down the hall. He hoped that Charles was asleep by now; Erinle had to use a stronger concentration of herbs to keep Charles' mind--and mouth-- quiet. If he mentioned Oyá's name aloud, her enemies would be able to find him and hurt him.

Charles was sound asleep beneath the purple covers on his bed when Erinle stepped back into the room. The *orisha* of herbs and healing stared down at the human's peaceful slumber, noticing how the age lines had relaxed on his face. Erinle sighed to himself. He wondered what, if anything, Charles had told his daughter; the night duty nurse on his wing mentioned that Charles had been having more lucid periods lately. For the sake of the *orisha* and Charles' protection under Oyá, it was imperative that his memories of the storm goddess be suppressed as much as possible. In the wrong hands, they could be used to harm Violet, and Oyá made it clear that Violet was to be kept from harm at all costs. Erinle was in no mood to tangle with the mighty *orisha*.

Erinle walked into the adjacent bathroom and ran tap water into the sink. Because one of the city's water sources was the Chattahoochee River, and since Erinle was associated with rivers (which is how he met his former wife, the river *orisha* Oshun), he could scry with the water to determine future events--or even current ones.

Erinle peered into the sink full of water and concentrated. Soon, images appeared of the occurrences in Charles Davidson's room for the past two hours. The healer *orisha* saw Charles being helped into the bathroom by a nurse, presumably to bathe; him getting dressed; him sitting by the window with his sketchpad and pencils, drawing with fervor and pausing only to occasionally stare out the window. Violet's arrival, and their stilted communication.

Erinle frowned when Violet abruptly rushed into the bathroom. Her face looked sad, as if she were about to cry. Humans got worked up over the silliest things. She exited the bathroom with reddened eyes, which confirmed Erinle's suspicion of crying. He watched her resume her conversation with her father, then turn at his, Erinle's, entrance.

STORMBRINGER

Erinle drained the sink and dried his hands on a nearby clean towel, trying to quell the anxiety roosting in his chest. Things were worse than he'd hoped. Charles was not only resisting the herbal concoctions that had been made for him, but he was speaking Oyá's name freely and remembering their dalliance so many moons ago. He knew how his former wife felt about her sister Oyá; Oshun would not tolerate Charles' existence, which would serve as a continuous reminder of her sister in this realm.

He sighed, straightened his tie, and left Charles's room altogether. Oshun's petulance was about to start an *orisha* war. He had to contact his brothers.

Erinle flashed into the forest near the Chattahoochee River. Despite still being dressed in his business casual attire and lab coat, his clothes remained unsoiled as he walked through the trees. The forest was his natural habitat, especially near rivers and streams. He inhaled deeply as he walked and wished that he were back in the forest, collecting herbs.

A rustle to his right caused Erinle to stop in his tracks. Soon, a man appeared through the branches, dressed in nothing but bright blue cloth loosely draped around his lower body. The man held a large bow in one hand; the other held a brace of rabbits tied together with a leather thong. He ducked beneath a large branch, careful not to catch the ends of the arrows that were tucked in the case strapped to his back. The man stopped when he saw Erinle. "Brother," the man greeted in surprise.

"Ochosi," Erinle replied. He nodded at the rabbits. "Good hunting, I see."

"Not really. The animals seem to be hiding for some reason. There is no storm on the horizon, so I'm not sure why that is."

"Oh, there's a storm brewing, alright, but not the type you mean. Have you seen Osain?"

"He's around here somewhere." Ochosi narrowed his eyes as he stared at his brother. "Why? What's wrong?"

"I'd rather wait to explain it to both of you, so I don't have to repeat myself."

"Very well."

The two brothers flashed to a deeper part of the forest. Osain was crouched before a stand of large-leafed stalks, breaking off leaves and stuffing them into a large sack. He turned when he heard the other two *orisha* approach.

"Brothers!" Osain regarded them with one brown eye and one clouded gray eye. "It has been some time since we were all together. To what do I owe this visit?"

"Erinle has some news," Ochosi answered.

"Very well." Osain rose, adjusting his green and white robes about his slim body with his one arm. He hopped with his one leg over to a nearby fallen log, where his crutch leaned against it. He sat and placed the sackful of leaves at his feet. Ochosi preferred to remain standing, though he leaned against the trunk of a nearby tree.

Erinle shoved his hands in his pockets and took a deep breath. "An *orisha* war is about to break out as a result of the descendants of the Lost Children."

Ochosi frowned. Osain blinked. "Excuse me?"

"One of the Lost Children has a descendant who is of Oyá's--and possibly Changó's--lineage. This descendant is a human woman who can call lightning and thunder at will. Her father was intimate with Oyá and when Oyá cut off further contact, the human lost his mind. He has been in a nursing home for the past five years, where I am able to keep an eye on him while posing as his human physician. Oyá owns the healthcare company that owns the nursing home, so that he is protected. However, he has recently been speaking her name aloud, which will bring him to the attention of those who would wish him and his progeny harm."

Ochosi fiddled with his bow while he and Osain digested this information. "So why are you involved, Erinle? These humans have nothing to do with you."

"Oyá was most insistent that her human, Charles, and his daughter, Violet, be protected at all costs."

"But if the woman can call lightning and thunder," Ochosi surmised, "then that means that she is indeed of Oyá and Changó's lineages. Yet you are willing to risk the wrath of Oshun by standing with Oyá?"

"I stand with right over wrong. Oshun has no reason to harm that woman other than sheer jealousy. I've heard talk that she has already tried to have the woman killed."

Osain's eyebrows rose to his shaved hairline. "By whom?"

"Some police officer who was said to serve Ogún."

"Great." Ochosi sighed. "I was hoping that Ogún wouldn't be involved but if Oshun was, I should have known better."

"So, now what?" Osain asked.

Ochosi straightened. "Now, we try to stop an *orisha* war before it starts. I will have a word with Eshú to figure out what else may have happened by now." He checked the string on his bow. "I, too, stand for justice. I never quite agreed with the banishment of the Lost Children to Earth. The potential consequences were too far-reaching to make such a rash and political decision."

"So what are you going to do? Are you going to fight? And for whom?"

"Ogún has never listened to reason where Oshun is concerned; it's going to take someone he trusts to get through to him. He's been one of my closest friends for millennia; the task falls to me." Ochosi pulled back on the bowstring to test its tightness and nodded in satisfaction. "As for fighting, I will protect the humans, as Oyá asked."

Osain fixed his brother with a thoughtful look from his good eye. "You would fight against your own? You would take the side of a human over an *orisha*?"

Ochosi returned the look with a steady one of his own. "I take the side of the wrongly persecuted. Whether that is *orisha* or human, is not for me to determine." He gripped his bow for better carriage. "Erinle, we will be in touch. I must find Ogún." With that, Ochosi flashed out of the forest.

.

FIVE

Oshun strode through the serene atmosphere of the day spa she owned, her high heels muffled in the thick carpet. She nodded and smiled at the clients as they shuffled to and from their treatments, their naked flesh encased in plush, butter yellow terry cloth robes and their feet in disposable yellow slippers. Staff members, neatly turned out in uniforms of yellow smocks and black slacks and shoes, attended to the clients with a diligence and joy that was a common feature in the spa's employees.

She was headed back to her office when she heard it. She paused, mid-stride, and concentrated. Yes, there it was again. Oyá's name, from the mouth of one of her humans. Oshun closed her eyes and traced the vocalization back to its source. Her eyes flew open. So, Oyá's pet human was speaking of their dalliance. Surely her sister wasn't so sloppy but if she were, so much the better. A slight smile played across Oshun's lips as she entered her office and sat behind her spacious desk. This time, she would not contact Ogún; he had failed her once already. No, it was like the humans liked to say: never send a god to do a goddess's job.

STORMBRINGER

Goldie, the head cosmetologist of
Butterfly, an upscale hair salon, pulled into the
underground garage of her condominium building
in Atlantic Station. She'd had a long day of
demanding clients, including an up-and-coming
singing trio, the wife *and* mistress of one of the
Atlanta Falcons, and a local news celebrity. She
strode across the carpeted floors of her living
room, kicking off her wedge-heeled sandals with
a sigh of relief and tossing her work bag onto the
couch. She loosened the button on her designer
skinny jeans, which she quickly shucked in her
bedroom in favor of more comfortable
sweatpants and slouchy socks.

On her way back to the kitchen, she
stopped in the third bedroom, which she'd
converted to an altar room. She entered the
room, as always lifted by the butter yellow walls.
Goldie cast a practiced eye over the space that
paid homage to Oshun, the *orisha* she served.
The five yellow roses--five was Oshun's sacred
number--she'd placed there that morning were
holding up well, and both the vase of flowers and
a brand new bottle of perfume sat atop a gold
lamé runner, which itself laid upon a deep yellow
tablecloth printed with butterflies. There was also

102

a small, sample jar of honey that Goldie had received in a Christmas gift basket and a necklace of amber and gold beads with a large pendant worked into the form of a butterfly, its wings outstretched. A small plate of five sweet potato slices, drizzled in honey and sprinkled with cinnamon, was in front of the roses.

Goldie nodded to herself, satisfied that all seemed in order. She lit a cone of honeysuckle-scented incense, then sank to the large gold floor pillow in front of the altar. "Oshun, I am here, great goddess," she spoke aloud. "Speak to me, so that I may serve you best." She closed her eyes and regulated her breathing. The sweet scent of honey surrounded her, as if the very air she breathed was made of it. A repetitive, slow tap at the single window in the room made Goldie open her eyes: a fat bumblebee kept flying into the glass.

Goldie received a series of impressions in her mind: Elderly people, some with canes, some with walkers, some in wheelchairs. Employees in nursing scrubs. A large room with someone calling out Bingo numbers. A hospital--no, some sort of nursing home. A pine tree waving in the wind. Goldie received another impression which gave her pause, but she squelched her unease and paid attention to the vision. When the scent of honey faded, Goldie rose and left the altar room, closing the door behind her. She had to process her latest vision and figure out how to do what Oshun wanted done.

***

"Hi, Goldie" one of the nurses sang as Goldie entered Pine Breezes Assisted Living Facility with her two assistants in tow. "The natives are getting restless, waiting for you to arrive."

"Tell them that good things come to those who wait," Goldie teased. She hefted her portable manicure table in one hand and adjusted her duffel bag full of nail polishes and other nail necessities in the other. Her assistants carried portable shampoo bowls and chairs, as well as other hair care implements.

"They're waiting for you in your usual room." The nurse waited for Goldie and her crew to sign in, then led her down two halls toward a small recreation room. A group of elderly women, denizens of the facility, sat in chairs and looked hopefully at the door when Goldie walked in. She was met with a range of smiles, from toothless to denture-bright white. Goldie smiled in return as she set up her styling chair and instruments, while her assistants set up two shampoo bowls and a manicure table. As soon as she was ready, a reed-thin woman with a corona of cottony white hair lowered herself into the chair. A magazine was clutched in her bony hand. "I want some hair," she announced as she leaned back in the chair.

Goldie's eyes danced with amusement. "Hair, Mrs. Oviedo?"

"Yeah." Mrs. Oviedo nodded. "Jack Connelly in Room 43 asked me to dinner tonight. I gotta look good." She flipped to a page in the magazine that she'd carefully bookmarked with an old lottery number printout. "Can you make me look like Beyoncé?"

Goldie bit her lip to keep from laughing aloud at the earnest look on Mrs. Oviedo's face. Given that the woman was at least forty years older, fifty pounds lighter, four shades darker, and five inches shorter than the mega popular singer, not even Oshun herself could work such a miracle. "I think Mr. Connelly will like you the way you are, with a little boost. If you looked like Beyoncé, how would he recognize you?"

Mrs. Oviedo pondered that for a moment. "Good point," she conceded. "Well, can you give me a nice perm, maybe a blue rinse? And I want to get my nails done, too."

"I got you, Mrs. O." Goldie reclined the back of the chair and began to shampoo the elder woman's hair.

Four hours later, there was only one person left, and she only wanted a manicure and pedicure. Goldie used that downtime to use the restroom and implement her plan. After leaving the restroom, she crept down the hall toward the residential rooms, jumping into a darkened room as a pair of nurses walked by. When the hallway was once again clear, she followed the room numbers until she arrived at the one that housed Charles Davidson.

Goldie entered the room, her eyes adjusting to the bright light streaming through the window. She looked around the small room, but no Charles. She peered into the adjacent bathroom: empty. She turned to leave when a doctor entered the room. Goldie cursed to herself. She hadn't counted on any of the medical staff stopping by, since most of the residents were at various recreational activities at this time of the day. She only took a chance on finding Charles because Oshun gave the impression that he didn't socialize much, preferring to stay in his room. The doctor, in his aqua-patterned tie and blindingly white lab coat, had the type of no-nonsense look that didn't bode well for Goldie if she didn't make up a good lie as to why she was there.

"Who are you, and why are you in here?" Erinle demanded.

"I, uh, was visiting my uncle, Charles. But he's not here."

"Uncle?" Erinle regarded the woman closely, noticing the blonde hair and yellow smock, obvious makeup, and glittery earrings. "There is no mention of any other relatives in this patient's chart." He used his *orisha* senses and picked upon on something..."You serve Oshun," he hissed in a low voice.

"I..."

"Leave this place!" Erinle used his powerful telepathic skills to reach into Goldie's mind.

Goldie's eyes went unfocused, her mouth slack. "It's time for me to leave," she said in a dull monotone. She walked toward the doorway; Erinle stepped aside to let her pass. He peeked out the door and watched as Goldie disappeared down the hall and around a corner.

Once he was alone in the room, Erinle let his anger come to the surface. He was glad he'd had the presence of mind to schedule a last-minute exam for Charles outside of the facility; he'd had a feeling that Oshun would make her move sooner than later, and his feeling turned out to be correct. But surely Oshun was not that stupid? There was only one way to find out. He flashed out of the room.

Oshun scrubbed her hands vigorously beneath the running water as she gazed into the large window of the surgical suite. Her human guise as a plastic surgeon was an amusing one for her, as she never tired of the lengths humans were willing to undergo in order to achieve generalized standards of beauty. She had already performed a tummy tuck and a gluteal implant that day, and she was about to do a breast augmentation. A flash of light behind her caught her attention and she turned to see Erinle, her former husband, also clad in surgical scrubs.

"Erinle! To what do I owe the pleasure?" She noticed his glower. "Or displeasure, as seems to be the case?"

"I intercepted your servant, Oshun. You have gone too far!"

Oshun blinked and turned her attention back to her hands. How did Erinle find out? "I have no idea what you're ranting about, Erinle. What servant?"

"Don't play coy with me, Oshun. I know your tricks. Why did you send one of your human servants to harm the descendant of Oyá?"

"I did no such thing." She shut off the faucets with her elbows and dried her hands on a sterile towel.

"Oh? Then why did I find one--a woman, no less--in the descendant's room, when she had no cause to be there?"

"How do you know she had no cause? She was probably a relative."

"He has no relatives other than Oyá's descendant, and the woman was a beautician who comes to the facility twice a month to style the hair of some of the residents." He crossed his arms across his chest. "What have you done?"

"I don't know why you're accusing me of such a terrible thing." Oshun lowered her lashes and looked up through them at Erinle's implacable expression.

Erinle snorted as he looked down upon the butterflies scattered across Oshun's surgical cap.

"Don't even try it, Oshun. Your coquetry doesn't work on me. I'm not Ogún."

Oshun dropped her submissive act and glared at Erinle. "What I'm doing is no business of yours, Erinle. You would do well to stay out of matters that do not concern you."

"They concern me more than you know. Now, I must ask you to cease and desist with whatever plan you've concocted."

"You're asking me to cease and desist?" She laughed aloud. "Seriously? I do not answer to you any longer, Erinle. Not that I ever did."

Erinle tilted his head to concede the point. "Yet and still, it is best for you to step away from this human. The results of carrying through your plans could be catastrophic."

Oshun sucked her teeth as she noticed the patient wheeled into the operating room, where the nurses and anesthesiologist prepared to sedate her. "Who's going to stop me?" she tossed over her shoulder as she pushed past Erinle and entered the OR, hands held in the air to avoid contamination.

Erinle could only stare at her retreating form as he reluctantly realized that he would have to take a more active part in the protection of Oyá's descendant, and that his role in this dustup would not be long for exposure--which could possibly set off yet another *orisha* war, on top of the one already brewing.

SIX

I browsed the aisles of Libations, a liquor store in my neighborhood. Unlike other stores that gave off a seedy vibe, this store was well-lit and had an extensive inventory of liquor, wine, and beer. The staff were both friendly and knowledgeable and the store carried items at different price points so that everyone had the opportunity to afford something. After the day I'd had, I needed something to calm my nerves. The piped-in, drum-heavy music pulsated through the invisibly mounted speakers and was oddly soothing.

"Have you found what you are looking for?"

I almost dropped the bottle of a red wine blend that I'd been examining. "I, uh, I'm just looking." I eyed the man who'd snuck up on me. He was rather tall and well-built beneath the red and white striped shirt and khaki pants. The red bow tie and suspenders added a quirky touch. "I didn't even hear you come up behind me."

"Really? I usually get the opposite." His brown eyes glinted in amusement behind his gold-rimmed glasses. He nodded at the bottle of wine in her hand. "That's a pretty popular bottle. It just came out last week."

"Yeah? I am always on the lookout for something new to try."

"I urge you to do so. I'm glad that I took a chance on it and placed an order. Customers really enjoy it."

"So you're the buyer here?" I had only seen the sales staff, so I had no idea who was in upper management for the store.

"Actually, I own the store." He stuck out a hand. "Drummond Aruwo-Ara."

"Violet Davidson." As we shook hands, a glint of gold at Drummond's wrists caught my attention. "Those are cool cufflinks. Are those..." I leaned in for a closer look, "axes?"

Drummond cast a cursory glance at the cufflinks. "Thank you, and yes. Double-headed axes. Do you live around here?"

"Yes, not far. I stop in here at least once a week. I've never seen you here, though."

"I travel a lot, but I have some business to attend to here that requires me to stay in one place for a bit." Drummond smiled, revealing a smile that was a dentist's fantasy. "May I show you some other items that may pique your interest?"

I followed him to the rear of the store, where Drummond led me to a small rack filled with an array of reds and whites from the same vintner. "This is a newly established vineyard in South Africa," he explained as he slid a bottle of red wine from the display. He turned the label toward me. "This is a pinotage. I find it to be dry yet lush, with plum, blackberry, and licorice notes." The chimes over the shop door rang and Drummond looked up and over the shelves. He was quite tall, around 6'4" or 6'5", so he could easily see across the tops of the shelves to the front of the store. "Hello, I'll be right with you," he called. He turned his attention back to me and continued. "This is excellent but this," he retrieved a bottle of white wine from the display, "is a life-changer."

As Drummond extolled the virtues of the bottle of Chardonnay, I felt myself drawn to him. Not in a sexual way; he was old enough to be my dad. But something about him felt familiar and comfortable. I relaxed for the first time in weeks as he selected two more bottles of wine for me. I followed him back up to the register, where he rang up my purchase and wrapped the bottles against breakage with ceremony, putting them into a red, twine-handled bag with a flourish. "Here you are," he said as he slid the bag toward me. "That should set you up for a bit."

"Thanks a lot. The way my life has been going, I'll need every drop."

"If you need more, you have only to return. I will take care of you."

I smiled at the protective tone in his voice, even as I wondered about it. It was as if his words had some sort of double meaning...but that was nuts. I'd never met Drummond before in my life, and he didn't know me like that. "Will do." I left the shop with more spring in my step that I'd had when I arrived.

***

Ochosi flashed inside a dimmed building. The stench of cordite permeated the air and his nostrils twitched in offense. Piercing sounds of gunfire echoed throughout the long hallway. Men and women stood in individual booths as they worked on their gun marksmanship; some were taking shots; others were reloading their weapons; still others were breaking down and cleaning their guns after a session of effort.

Ochosi concentrated on the instructor, clad in black cargo pants, combat boots, and a dark green T-shirt that stretched across his broad shoulders. The T-shirt was emblazoned with the name and logo of the combination gun shop and weapons school. The matching cap sat squarely atop his head as he strode in precise steps up and down the narrow corridor, stopping here and there to give correction or praise to a student.

The instructor paused slightly and turned to look over his shoulder. His eyes widened behind the protective glasses. He turned completely around and walked toward Ochosi with purpose, removing his bright orange ear plugs as he did. "Ochosi," Ogún greeted his old friend with an arm clasp. "What brings you to the human realm?"

Ochosi returned the greeting. "I came to speak to you of an urgent matter."

"Let me guess: you've heard about the descendants of the Lost Children and are here to try and make me see the error of my ways, for attempting to help Oshun." He rolled his eyes. "Sorry, friend. As the humans like to say, that ship has already sailed."

Ochosi shoved his hands inside the pockets of his loose-fitting khaki pants. "At least you're admitting that you are involved."

"Of course I'm involved. Oshun asked for my help."

"But was it your place to give it?"

Ogún sucked his teeth and nodded at another instructor, who took over the class. Ogún gestured for Ochosi to follow him, and they went down the narrow hallway to another, larger hallway that led to one of the two entrances to the gun shop. Ochosi marveled at the array of weapons available and lingered in front of a mechanical crossbow. The two *orisha* ended up in the office. Ogún sat behind a large metal desk that housed a flat screen monitor, keyboard, and stacks of papers. "Now, what were you saying, Ochosi?"

"I was saying that perhaps you should have left well enough alone. It's bad enough that Oshun is trying to battle her sister..."

Ogún cut him off with an angry slash of his hand. "Oshun had managed to put the sordid issue of Oyá and Changó behind her. This descendant of theirs would hurt her even more."

"Ogún," Ochosi sighed with a shake of his head. "This is between Oshun and Oyá. And it will not bring Oshun back into your bed, or your life."

Ogún's face turned red with rage. "Watch your mouth," he warned.

"Oshun is using you for her own purposes. She has never hesitated because she counts on your loyalty, misguided or no." Ochosi leaned forward in earnest. "This will not end well for you, old friend. Especially when Changó gets involved."

"You think I fear Changó?" Ogún's large hands clenched into fists the size of small boulders. "I fear no *orisha*!"

Ochosi rubbed his temples in frustration. He loved Ogún like a brother, but he was too often too stubborn for his own good. "Aside from the fact that he's your half-brother and it would break Yemajá's heart if you fought each other, there is the matter of him being one of the strongest, most powerful *orisha* in our pantheon."

"I am the *orisha* of battle," Ogún yelled, thumping his chest for emphasis.

"And Changó is the *orisha* of war. There is a difference, and you know it." Ochosi gave Ogún a knowing look. "And now it is time for you to remove yourself from this situation. Let it resolve itself."

Ogún shook his head. "It's too late for that."

"Why?" When Ogún remained silent, Ochosi tried to quell his apprehension. "Why, Ogún?"

"Things have been set in motion that cannot be undone."

"By whom?" More silence. "What have you done, Ogún?"

Ogún told him.

Ochosi rushed out of the gun shop to find Erinle. What he thought might be a potentially bad situation was about to get much worse.

SEVEN

Changó flashed into Olorun's tent. The Wise Father, who was in deep conversation with Yeguá, looked up in surprise. "Changó!"

"*Baba*," Changó greeted. He nodded at Yeguá, though he kept a healthy distance; for all of his strengths, he was afraid of death. "Yeguá."

"Hello, Changó." Yeguá's eyes twinkled with mirth. She was well aware of Changó's fear. She looked at Olorun. "We can continue this later, *Baba*."

"Yes, yes. I think Changó has something urgent to discuss."

Yeguá rose, her pink robes swirling gracefully about her slim figure. Her long braids swayed down her back, ornamented with cowrie shells and ribbons of pink cloth woven into the braids. She flashed out of the tent. Olorun turned his attention back to Changó. "What is it, my son? You look distressed."

"Not really, *Baba*. More like...contemplative." Changó started to sit in the chair recently vacated by Yeguá, but decided against it. Instead, he sank down into the chair next to it. He adjusted his red robes with the white, double-head drum pattern around his chiseled physique. "I made contact today. With my descendant."

"Oh?" Olorun knew that Changó moved fast, but he was still surprised. More so, since he figured Changó to ignore the brouhaha surrounding the descendants of the Lost Children. He had a tendency to be rather self-absorbed.

"Yes. I didn't want to believe the rumors that were told to me by *Iya* Yemajá and *Baba* Aganjú, or even Oyá, but I decided to look into it myself." His gaze took on a far-seeing quality. "I felt her essence, *Baba*. She is indeed of my lineage. I also felt Oyá's essence as well."

"Did she recognize you? I am told that the woman was able to manifest thunder by thinking about it."

Changó shook his head. "No. Her senses are not yet evolved, though I can tell that she felt something familiar about me. Humans tend to relax around people with whom they feel comfortable. She simply knows me now as the proprietor of a local wine shop in her neighborhood."

Olorun nodded. "You realize that this makes the human woman very formidable, should she gain complete manifestation and control of her powers."

"I agree. Which is why I will be monitoring her closely, in case she needs my assistance."

"Hmm. Are you aware that Oyá has had protection in place for the woman for quite some time?"

"I would expect nothing less from her. She is not called the Mother of Nine for no reason. She is fiercely protective of that and those she deems hers."

"Are you also aware that Oshun is not pleased by this turn of events?"

Changó sighed. "I am not, but I am not surprised. Oshun does not like competition in any form, especially when it comes from her sister." He cocked his head and regarded Olorun. "Has Oshun tried to harm the woman?"

"There have been disturbances on Earth to suggest that," Olorun admitted.

A furrow of concern creased Changó's brow. "Was Ogún involved?" At Olorun's silence, the concern turned into a glower. "Of course. He remains Oshun's faithful lap dog, even when she runs back to me." He shook his head to rid himself of the negative thoughts. "Since the woman seems to be unharmed still, I take it that he did not succeed?" At Olorun's nod, Changó turned pensive. "Of course, Oshun is not one to give up without a fight, which means she will probably try to employ one of her human servants to do the job. Which will put her squarely at odds with Oyá; that is a battle Oshun will not win. Not that that has stopped her before." Changó rubbed his large hand across his face, letting his weariness and anxiety show for the first time. "I will have to stop Oshun. She will listen to me where she will not heed others."

A secret smile played across Olorun's lips. "I don't think you need to engage in this wave of battle, Changó. There is yet another ally of which you are unaware."

"Really? Who, *Baba*?" At Olorun's silence, still with that secret smile, Changó returned the smile with a large one of his own. "Ah, well, that just makes things more interesting! I shall have to spend more time in the human realm to, as the humans say, keep my ear to the ground." He rose and left the tent in good spirits.

Olorun sighed deeply and turned back to the scrying bowl on his table, where he and Yeguá had been discussing the next humans to enter the afterlife. If Changó knew what he and Yeguá knew, he'd realize that his increased time in the human realm would become even more crucial.

EIGHT

I pressed the button on my key fob and the car alarm chirped to life with a flash of headlights. I was dog tired, boss; the museum had a major fundraising gala in three days and I had stayed late at work--at the behest of my boss--to tie up any loose ends. It was one of the three major fundraisers the museum hosted per year, and had brought in at least $300,000 for the past five years. Having it go off less than perfectly was not an option.

My steps were slow as I trudged up the sidewalk from the parking space I managed to find, two blocks away. The street was quiet at this time of evening, but it was a quiet neighborhood anyway. School-aged children and younger were either already in bed or on their way. Dinners were mostly done and people were settling into preparations for the next day at work or school.

As I approached my apartment building, I heard footsteps behind me. Years of city living made me instantly apprehensive, though living in the south for the past six years had dulled that city survival edge to a degree. Still, I knew better than to let someone walk up behind me unawares. I turned to see a curvaceous woman with a big smile and dyed blond hair approach. She was dressed casually in form-fitting jeans and a yellow T-shirt beneath a denim jacket bedazzled with gold crystals. The crystals on the jacket matched the rhinestones in her dangly hoop earrings. "Excuse me," the woman said as she walked closer. "Could you tell me which way Forsyth Avenue is?" She brandished her cell phone. "I think I put the wrong address into Apple Maps."

"Sure. You're not that far. You just need to..." I pointed in the direction that she should go, which caused me to turn my back briefly on the woman.

Big mistake.

Pain exploded across the back of my head and I fell to my knees with the sound of angry bees buzzing in my ear, which I chalked up to the head injury. My keys and leather tote bag went flying. I saw droplets of blood hit the pavement below me and knew that I would at least need stitches, if I was lucky enough not to have a brain bleed. I managed to turn and look at the woman, whose smile had turned into something more sinister. "Who...what...who are you?"

The woman swung a coin-filled athletic sock at her side. The nubby white cotton was stained with blood. My blood. "I'm here to right a wrong, praise Oshun."

She raised her foot to kick me while I was down--in my haze I somehow noticed her metallic gold leather trendy ankle boots. I threw out a hand to stop her. Lightning shot out and nicked her in the arm, since she dodged the bolt at the last minute. She rolled to the side and stared at her burned jacket sleeve in disgust. She stripped off the jacket and tossed it aside. I looked up and down the street for help but it was empty. I couldn't even find anyone looking out of the window.

I opened my mouth to scream but the woman threw out a hand. A stream of something sticky and sweet shot out and splashed me from head to toe. Honey, from the smell of it. I was trying to wipe some of it from my eyes when a swarm of bees surrounded me. The honey attracted them and I screamed aloud as I was stung multiple times, even as I tried to figure out how and why bees were out at this time of night; they were daytime insects, as far as I knew.

A crack of lightning lit up the cloudless sky, followed by a deep boom of thunder. I was hurt, confused, blinded by honey of all things, and getting madder by the second. My temper flared and so did a flash of light around my body. There was a sizzling sound, then the swarm disappeared. The smell of burnt honey filled the air as I managed to open one honey-crusted eye. The sidewalk around me was littered with the blackened carcasses of fried bees.

The woman had backed away, her eyes rounded with fear. "What...how..." she stammered.

I staggered to my feet. A wave of dizziness almost made me fall back down, but I stayed upright. "Who the hell are you, and why did you hit me?"

"Because you shouldn't be alive," another voice said.

I turned to the source of the new voice and saw a beautiful woman standing there. Her deep yellow robes floated about her curvy figure; the halter cut of the torso emphasized her significant cleavage and bare shoulders. A high split on one side exposed her toned legs. The color of her robes set off her deep brown skin. Her thick, dark hair expanded from her head in a crinkly Afro that would have rivaled Angela Davis's. Her expression belied her beauty; indeed, she looked at me as if I were a bug that needed stepping on.

The blonde woman on the sidewalk fell to her knees in...awe? "Oshun," she breathed as she prostrated herself on the sidewalk.

Oshun paid the woman no attention; her dark brown eyes remained fixed on me. She tapped a folded fan against her thigh. "I do not understand how you came to be. Well, actually I do, kind of. Still," she shrugged an elegant shoulder, "just because you are my sister's pet project doesn't mean you are a viable one."

The air around us became charged with an energy that was unlike any I'd ever experienced. It was difficult for me to breathe. I shook my head, which set off even more waves of pain. My stomach twisted like I was about to vomit; I was afraid I had a concussion. "What?" I whispered. "I don't understand."

Oshun huffed in exasperation. "Come on. From all accounts you are a rather smart human. Which means you already know about my sister and her quest to protect you from those who might harm you."

My research was starting to come back to me as I cradled my aching head in one of my hands. Oshun, the younger sister of Oyá. She was the *orisha* of love and harmony. She also held a long-standing grudge against Oyá over the latter's relationship with the thunder *orisha* Changó. I cursed silently to myself; things were looking worse and worse for me. "Look," I panted, "whatever beef you have with Oyá, that's between y'all. Leave me out of it."

Oshun flicked open her fan with a practiced twitch of her wrist. In the glow of the streetlights, the peacock feather pattern seemed to glow in an otherworldly fashion. She fanned herself with languid strokes, even though the temperature was around fifty-five degrees. She clucked her tongue in derision. "No, human, I daresay that you are now a key part of this 'beef' between me and my sister." She cocked her head to the side. "What is a 'beef'? My sisters and I never raised livestock, so it couldn't mean that."

This conversation was surreal. "A 'beef' is a disagreement."

"Ah." Oshun nodded. "Well, as I said, this 'beef' would not have occurred had it not been for poor choices my sister made decades ago. Lying with humans is beneath *orisha*."

"If you say so," I muttered.

"But I did say so," she purred. There was no comfort in that tone of voice. "And I was not alone. There were other *orisha* who felt the same; enough of us to cause the humans, with which some had engaged in intimate relationships, to be banished to Earth. We thought that was the end of it. Then someone like you comes along."

"Like me?"

"My sister has not explained what you are?" Oshun chuckled--a chilling sound. "You are a descendant of the *omo sǫnu olorun*."

"The who?"

"The Lost Children of the Gods," Oshun retorted with much attitude. "Don't you know anything? Maybe you're not as smart as people say."

I vaguely remembered Navasha saying something about these Lost Children, but I was too busy concentrating on not throwing up to recall all the details. "The Lost Children were humans who had sex with *orisha* and were banished to Earth because some orisha were afraid that these humans would gain godlike powers and usurp the balance of power among the *orisha*."

"As if a human could ever be as powerful as an *orisha*," Oshun sneered. She fanned herself faster. "Still, if any offspring were to have powers, they should be the offspring of *orisha* only. Such as my children, the Ibeji." She stopped fanning herself. "You should not have your powers. You are not *orisha*."

"It's not like I asked for them. I don't even know how I do...whatever it is I do."

Revulsion twisted Oshun pursed lips. "*Orisha* are created knowing which powers we have, and exactly how to harness our powers. In the hands of the untrained--especially an untrained human--the consequences could be dire. All the more reason for you to be eliminated." She closed her fan, and her eyes, and raised her arms in the air.

I cowered and covered my head with my arms, since I had no idea what she was about to do. The sudden clouds above crackled with lightning. Thunder rolled in an ominous rumble.

Oshun reopened her eyes to stare at the sky, then back at me. A trace of fear flashed across her face so quickly that I thought I must have imagined it. "So the rumors are true, then. I'd wondered if they'd been exaggerated."

I peeked from beneath an arm. "You were going to kill me based on unconfirmed intel? That's stupid."

The murderous look on Oshun's face made me wish I'd kept my mouth shut. "What is stupid, human, is you having powers that do not belong to you, and not knowing how to use those powers. And I don't need to confirm anything. I am *orisha*." She closed her eyes again and raised her arms even higher.

The air pulsed in a strange rhythm and I heard a loud rush of water in the distance. But from where? There was a fountain in the courtyard of a nearby shopping complex, but there wasn't enough water in it to make that much noise. No, this was the sound of a larger body of water rushing forth. Bu again, from where? The underground sewers? The thought of waste-laced, germ-infested sewer water washing over us was the final impetus my stomach needed. I bent over and upchucked what remained of the sandwich I'd eaten a few hours ago.

I wiped my mouth with the back of my hand and straightened in time to see a torrent of brownish water spilling across the paved streets and sidewalks, heading straight for us. Before I had a chance to fully process what I was seeing, a bolt of lightning struck the street in front of me. The tarmac crumbled into a hole, into which the raging waters spilled to flow harmlessly in the underground sewage system. I whipped around and saw the woman from my dream.

Oyá.

She stood behind me, her long, dark dreadlocks floating around her muscular shoulders in the energy-charged atmosphere. Her purple skirt hung from her waist in strips, revealing long, strong legs. She had to be over six feet tall, even in the flat-heeled sandals. A halter of closely sewn cowrie shells covered her torso, and her face was covered in a mask of palm fronds. In each hand was a sharp-looking machete that glowed with an otherworldly aura.

Oshun dropped her arms and opened her eyes once more. Her expression turned sour. "Sister."

"I told you what would happen if you tried to harm me or mine." The palm fronds fluttered with each word Oyá spoke. Her deep, melodious voice was ominous.

Oshun put her hands on her rounded hips. "You don't frighten me. I did what needed to be done, what you couldn't be counted on to do, because of your attachment to your precious humans."

"That attachment comes with a price, and unfortunately it is the humans who must pay."

"A price on a debt you should never have entered in the first place." Oshun spat on the ground. "We are *orisha*! We are beyond the comprehension of mere humans. Why act as if they deserve more, all because you and some other *orisha* couldn't control themselves!"

"This is not a black or white issue, Oshun. If you would just stop and think about the fallacy of your arguments..."

Oshun shrieked in petulant anger and flung her arms forward. A fresh deluge of water rushed forward from wherever it was coming from. The speed of the flow caused the hole in the pavement to quickly fill and spill over into the street. Rivulets of water poured down the street and into the gutters, as if there had been a massive rainfall.

Oyá pointed a machete in the air. Wind gathered, then whipped around us in a counterclockwise motion. The wind picked up the water and used it to form a moving wall around myself, Oyá , and Oshun. We were in the eye of a hurricane.

Oshun tried to gain control of the situation but Oyá was too strong. She pushed the hurricane up and away from us, sending it spinning across the treetops and buildings in the direction from which the flood came. The three of us stood facing each other. Oshun lifted an arm to try something else, her face a mask of anger and humiliation.

"Oshun, stop!"

We all turned to see a muscular man, dressed only in dark green robes draped around his lower body, striding toward us. His bald head gleamed in the streetlights and his face was set with purpose. Beside him was another man, slimmer but equally muscular, but with similar attire in a bright blue color. This man carried a large bow and a quiver of arrows on his back. His long dreadlocks were drawn back from his handsome, chiseled face and tied at the nape of his neck with a leather thong.

"Ogún." Oshun's face registered surprise, then pleasure, then confusion. "And Ochosi."

"Oshun," Ochosi greeted before turning to Oyá . "Mother of Nine."

"Hunter," Oyá replied with a nod.

"What are you two doing here?" Oshun asked. "Ochosi, you hardly ever visit the human realm."

Ochosi tilted his head in acknowledgement. "I felt it prudent to do so today."

The confusion on Oshun's face gave way to comprehension. "Oh, I get it. You and Ogún are here to do what the humans call 'an intervention'. Is that true?"

"Oshun, it is time to put this feud aside," Ogún said.

"Put it aside?" Oshun stared at Ogún as if he'd lost his mind. "Were you not the one who made it a point to apprise me of this human's," she gestured at me, "existence? Surely you knew how I would react."

"Well yes, but..."

"And you weren't too concerned with my putting anything aside when I rode you in my office."

Ogún hung his head beneath the knowing looks from the other two *orisha*. He lifted it to say, "Yes, I knew how you would react. I was angry at Changó and tried to assuage it by getting you involved. It was wrong of me."

"When are you not angry at Changó," Oyá muttered from behind her mask.

"Oh yes, let's not speak badly of your precious Changó," Ogún snapped at Oyá .

Oyá rolled her eyes to the heavens. "I can't believe you're still stuck on that. It's been millennia since that happened! I'm so sick of you whining about it at every possible turn."

STORMBRINGER

Ogún started to reply but Ochosi's hand on his arm silenced him. "Leave it be, Ogún," Ochosi warned in a low voice. "We have more pressing matters to attend to. Besides, you know what happened the last time you made her angry."

A sheepish look crossed Ogún's face. "I didn't think she'd be that mad. Not mad enough to create a category five hurricane."

"I can hear you, you know," Oyá said. "And I wasn't that mad at you; I was mad at Changó."

Ogún was incredulous. "So you destroyed New Orleans because you were angry at your lover?"

"He is my husband," Oyá snapped, "as well you know."

"He was my husband first," Oshun added with a snide smile.

Oyá pointed at her sister. "And Ogún was my husband first. Your point?" She watched Oshun's smile die with the reminder of her indiscretion with Ogún. "As for you," she pointed at Ogún, "you two were bickering, as usual when you are in the same place, and I was tired of it, on top of everything else. So I just snapped.

However, I did strengthen the storm to break the levees, to teach you a lesson."

"You what?" Ogún glowered at Oyá.

"I told you that your servants' work on those levees was inferior," Oyá snarled, "and you pouted. You were so sure that your metalwork would hold, and that your servants were so knowledgeable. Instead, your arrogance killed all those people."

"I didn't send a powerful hurricane to drown the city!"

"If you'd built those levees properly, the city would have sustained minor damage from the storm." Oyá shook her head in disgust. "Your ego will always be your downfall if you don't learn to harness it."

"Enough." Ochosi held up a hand to stop the argument. "While you sit here squabbling, the human of Oyá's lineage is injured."

***

I had sat down on the sidewalk during this *orisha* exchange. My head was hurting and my legs would no longer support me. I looked up at the good-looking, bare-chested orisha walking toward me with a sense of detachment, which I put down to my head injury and not any true nonchalance. I mean, it wasn't every day that a gorgeous African god approached you.

The *orisha* called Ochosi knelt in front of me. "What ails you, child?"

"My head. The woman hit me pretty hard." Ochosi's close proximity wasn't helping matters; in fact, the presence of four *orisha* in the same place was making the atmosphere feel very strange. All that godly essence was too concentrated for a mere human to deal with. But I hadn't hit my head hard enough to voice that opinion. I was learning that when it came to the *orisha*, silence was indeed golden.

Ochosi looked over to where the blonde woman was still prostrate on the ground. Ochosi rose and strode over to her. "Woman! Who are you?"

The woman looked up and sat back on her heels at Ochosi's appearance in front of her. "I...I'm Goldie," she managed to get out.

Ochosi's keen *orisha* senses were piqued. "You serve Oshun," he said with yet another frown.

"Yes," Goldie nodded.

"She sent you to do harm to this woman?"

"I..." Goldie looked to Oshun for help, but the river goddess ignored her.

STORMBRINGER

Oshun reopened her fan. "The woman serves me. I asked her to do my bidding, she tried, she failed. You all saved the day. Can we go now?" The boredom in Oshun's voice was at odds with her tense posture.

Ochosi shook his head. "You cannot expect to leave here without consequence."

Oshun looked Ochosi up and down. "The only one who can judge or punish me is Olodumare herself. And you are not she."

Ochosi sighed, then closed his eyes. There was another flash of light and Erinle appeared. He opened his mouth to greet the other *orisha*, then noticed me and Goldie. "Violet." he said with no little surprise.

Seriously? "Dr. Inle?" I didn't know what was more shocking: that a god was literally taking care of my father, or that my father seemed to know that he was a god, despite the human disguise.

"And...Goldie?"

Ochosi looked from me to Goldie, and back to Erinle. "You know these two, brother?"

"Violet is the descendant of Oyá, of whom I spoke earlier. She is also the daughter of Oyá's former consort. Goldie was an interloper at the nursing facility where Violet's father resides."

I somehow managed to focus my doubled vision on the woman they called Goldie. "You tried to hurt my dad?"

"Yes, Goldie. You tried to do harm to my consort?" Oyá's voice dripped with menace. The blades of her twin machetes flashed in the street light beams.

The fear on Goldie's face was palpable. "I...I didn't do anything to him. I don't even remember being at a nursing home, or meeting your dad."

The other *orisha* turned to look at Erinle. He shrugged. "I altered her memory and compelled her to leave the facility. Charles was absent from the facility at that time, so he was not there for her to carry out whatever plan Oshun gave her." He looked back at Goldie. "I see that I will need to do so again."

"You can't do that," Oshun protested. "You could mess up her mind if you do it too much!"

"I thought that the concerns of humans were beneath you?" Oyá asked sweetly.

"She's useful. Do you know how hard it is to find a good human servant these days?"

I looked over at Goldie, who looked as if she'd been slapped. My guess was that she had a lot of love for Oshun, but clearly the reverse wasn't true. How she could serve, or whatever, a goddess that was so self-centered was beyond me. Maybe there was a part of her personality that resonated with Oshun, and vice versa. I wasn't sure how this whole servant/*orisha* thing worked. Yet another question I had for Navasha.

Erinle simply shook his head and approached Goldie. "Goldie, look at me."

Goldie screwed her eyes shut and shook her head as well. "No. No way!" Her earrings swung violently.

"Goldie."

"No! You can't make me!"

A zap of energy touched Goldie's chest, and she gasped aloud. Her eyes flew open and Erinle began the process of altering her memories. The other *orisha* looked at Oyá, who'd sent the bolt. She shrugged. "What? We've been here long enough. I just sped things along."

Erinle stepped away from Goldie, who turned and walked back down the street from the direction she'd come. "She won't remember any of this," he said.

"Good." Oyá came over to me and looked down. "I am proud of you, daughter. You fought well, all things considered."

"Uh, thank you." I tried to see beyond the fronds on the mask, but they effectively hid her face. I wondered what she looked like. Was she pretty, like Oshun?

"You must learn to harness your powers; right now, their unpredictability could hurt both yourself and others. My servants will assist you."

Servants? Plural? "That would be great, thanks." My stomach heaved again and I threw up near her sandaled feet.

Concern crossed Oyá's face. "She is very injured. Erinle?"

Erinle came over to me and placed his strong hands on my head. My headache eased to a more manageable level, then disappeared altogether. My stomach stayed where it needed to be. My vision cleared. I was healed.

I touched the back of my head: no pain. I looked at my hand: no blood. "Wow. Hey, thanks!"

Amusement creased the corners of Erinle's eyes as he gave a half-bow of acknowledgment. "You are quite welcome. I didn't think it prudent that you visit a human hospital, as they would ask many questions to which you would not have sufficient answers. Then there would be the involvement of the police." He looked over at Ogún and Ochosi.

Ogún raised his hands in surrender. "Don't look at me. That soldier who attacked Violet, he was a new servant. Too hotheaded, even for me." He glanced at me. "He got what he deserved, if he couldn't defeat you with surprise on his side."

Wow. A nice reminder that I'd killed someone, even if it was in self-defense. Stay classy, Ogún.

Oshun huffed in exasperation. "If we're done with this little feel-good party, then I must go." She glared at the other four *orisha*. "I won't forget this." She left in a bright flash of light.

Oyá, Ogún, Ochosi and Erinle stared at the spot where she once stood. "You know that she will not stop," Ochosi said.

"Especially if there are other descendants," Oyá added.

Erinle opened his mouth to speak, but thought better of it. "Well, we will address that if and when the time comes." He looked at Ochosi and Ogún. "Come, brother, and Ogún; let us be gone from this place." To Oyá he said, "I will continue to keep a watch on your Charles."

"I appreciate it." Oyá gave a deep nod of thanks before turning her attention to me. "As for you, little one, it is time for you to get some rest."

Before I had time to reply, I was enveloped in a flash of light. That was the last thing I remembered before darkness overtook me.

NINE

I woke up to the sun streaming through my bedroom window. The light hurt my eyes but my head was fine. I sat up and fumbled with the strings on the blinds, shutting out the light.

I laid back down and looked at the ceiling. Last night, I'd been in the presence of five *orisha* and lived to tell the tale--not that I would be telling anyone but Navasha about this. Most people went their entire lives not even knowing about the *orisha*, much less seeing them. Oyá herself had been there, just as she appeared to me in my dream. She called me her child, just as she did in my dream. Another human saw them too, even though she probably wouldn't remember any of it. I wasn't crazy.

I slid into my fuzzy slippers and shuffled to my kitchen. While I waited for my coffee to brew, there was a knock at my front door. I opened it; it was Navasha.

She cast a critical eye over me. "You seem well."

"I am." The wording of her statement was interesting. "How much do you..."

"Oyá visited me in another vision, and told me to come by and check on you. But that was it." Her eyes twinkled with amusement at my puzzled expression. "I'll leave it to you to fill in the details." She held up a large white paper bag emblazoned with the logo of a popular fast food restaurant. "I brought biscuits."

Over sausage biscuits, hash browns, and coffee, I told Navasha what happened the night before. She listened with interest and was quiet when I was done.

"You were not only in the physical presence of the mighty Oyá, but also of four other *orisha*." She sighed in awe. "I'm jealous."

"Don't be. It's not all it's cracked up to be. It was very intense."

"As can be expected, when you have that many *orisha* in one place." She cradled her coffee mug in her hands. "So Oshun was trying to kill you because she didn't think you should have the powers of an *orisha*?"

"Pretty much. She said something about how she was against human/*orisha* relationships from jump, and was one of the *orisha* who convinced Olo...Oduma..."

"Olodumare," Navasha corrected. "The Supreme Creator. God, to use a Judeo-Christian analogy, though Olodumare is female."

"Yeah, her. Oshun helped convince Olodumare to banish those humans to Earth. Apparently, my dad and Oyá had a thing back in the day. He told me as much, though I doubt if he really understood what he was telling me." I looked down into the milky coffee in my own mug. "I think that being with her made him literally lose his mind."

"Unfortunately, that could be a byproduct of having a relationship with an *orisha*. Their power is too much for us mortals, which is why most *orisha* only visit during a meditation or vision. It's safer for humans. That's why it's very impressive that you are sitting there, unscathed."

"That we know of," I joked.

Navasha shook her head. "No. I'm serious. You would have already shown signs of being diminished in some way, had their essence had any effect on you."

Which brought me to one of the questions I had for Navasha. "How does this whole servant thing work? How did you choose, or were tapped, to serve Oyá?"

"Part of it was my personality. In my younger days I was quite the firebrand." Navasha smiled at the memory. "I believed in fighting back, and standing up for the less fortunate. I

149

had the foolhardy bravery of youth. But another part was just reading about the *orisha* in general and being drawn to Oyá, for some reason." She shifted in her chair to a more comfortable posture. "I had long since left the Baptist church of my upbringing and was in my experimental phase. I'd dabbled in Buddhism, other eastern religions, the Baha'i faith, and even read the Qur'an, though Islam wasn't my particular cup of tea.

"One day, some years ago, I was reading a book and it mentioned Oyá's areas of dominion: lightning, storms, battle, commerce, change, ancestors, and transition. I'd just inherited The Eggplant from my aunt, who'd recently passed. She didn't have any children, and I was her favorite niece. Anyway, the book said that one should make an offering to Oyá to ask for favor in business. I cut up some eggplant and put it on an altar, which was more like a multicolored scarf I'd laid atop a cabinet. I didn't really expect anything to happen. Then, I was contacted by a local news reporter about the shop and my aunt's death. That article brought in a lot of customers and while most came to just look around, enough people made purchases that I could keep the place open. Then I started selling the jewelry, and business got even better. From that day on, I continued to make offering to Oyá, and dedicated myself to her." She took a sip of coffee and added, "And I also was contacted by some random cousins through the site where I traced my family tree, and added some details that I'd been trying to find."

"Wow." I mulled over her story. "Should I make an altar to Oyá too?"

"It can't hurt. Though you already have her favor."

"Speaking of favor..." I hesitated while I tried to frame the question properly. "When I first told you about the hiking incident, and I told you about the thunder, you said that you would explain it later, that I wasn't ready to know at that time." I took a deep breath. "I think I'm ready to know now."

"Very well." Navasha drummed her fingers against her mug as she regarded me. "Remember when I told about the story of the Lost Children, and how the human consorts were banished to Earth, never to consort with the *orisha* again?" At my nod, she continued. "Well, you are..." She struggled to articulate her next statement. "When I asked you about your parents that day, I asked for a reason. You told me about your father, and how he was a consort with Oyá . You never mentioned your mother. That is important because...well, thunder is the province of the *orisha* Changó. Changó, as I have mentioned before, is the current husband of Oyá and is one of the major *orisha* in the pantheon. Where lightning goes, thunder follows." She gave me a piercing look. "I suspect that your being able to cause both is a direct result of both of your parents consorting with *orisha*: your father with Oyá, and your mother with Changó."

"But that's..." I started to say that was impossible but, given my mother's current situation, I couldn't be too sure.

Navasha noticed my uncertainty. "So, you have considered that possibility as well."

"Yeah. It came to me a short while ago. I wasn't ready to wrap my mind around it until last night. All that happened made me see things in a new light."

"If you are indeed Changó's descendant as well, then it will be a matter of time before he makes himself known, if he hasn't already."

"He's a war god, right?" At Navasha's nod, I asked, "Then why didn't he come last night, when Goldie attacked me? I could have used him then."

"You had Oyá, who is formidable in her own right. That is why Changó left Oshun for her. For both of them to have appeared would have been overkill. Plus, since you say that Ogún was there, things could have gotten very ugly, very quickly. Those two *orisha* do not get along at all, and with their women there, it would have gotten really bad. I wouldn't have put it past Oshun to manipulate the both of them as a means of taking the attention off her and her misdeeds, and Oyá would not have stood for that. No," she shook her head, "it was best that Changó did not appear."

"Would he ever come if I were in trouble?"

"That all depends on the magnitude of the trouble. I think that if it were serious enough, he'd come to handle matters himself. But from what I gather, he is content to delegate where necessary. Plus, he has Oyá to have his back, so he doesn't feel the urge to jump into battle unless it's something huge, or unless he is slighted to the point where he can't ignore it. His ego is massive." She took another sip of coffee. "I wonder," she mused, "if there are others like you?"

"Like me, how?"

"Children of parents who consorted with *orisha*."

"You think there are more?"

"I didn't know *you* existed for a long time," she said with a grin. "There is much more in this world than we know. I wouldn't be surprised if there are others. There are many *orisha*, and a whole lot of humans to boot."

This was too much to process, though I admitted to being intrigued by the possibility of finding more descendants of the *orisha*. It would be nice to have someone to talk to who really understood. Not that Navasha wasn't great, but she was only servant to an *orisha*; she didn't have any special powers to speak of. But then I thought about Goldie, and how she shot honey out of her hand. Was she a descendant too? Oshun called her a servant, but she could have been just saying that to be mean. Would Goldie be willing to talk to me about it? Would she even remember me? How thoroughly did Erinle wipe her mind?

Exhaustion washed over me. Navasha noticed and left, kissing me on the cheek before departure. We set a date for me to start learning more about my powers and how to harness them; Navasha said that she had some crystals

that would help me focus. I went back into my
room and crawled beneath the covers, and into
blissful sleep. Before I fell asleep, though, I could
have sworn that I heard the beating of drums.

***

Changó stepped away from the river in
satisfaction. "I want to thank you again for
healing her head," he said to Erinle.

Erinle waved a hand over the river
surface, allowing it to flow easily once again.
He'd used it to scry for Changó, who wanted to
check on Violet in the aftermath of her altercation
with Oshun's human servant Goldie. "Don't
mention it. She has a strong constitution, and a
hard head." He shot Changó a sly look. "Like
someone else I know."

"Ha ha." Changó folded his arms across
his chiseled chest. "Do you think Oyá's servant
was correct? That there are more descendants of
the Lost Children?"

"I wouldn't be surprised. But if there are,
that means that Oshun, and those who think like
her, won't rest until they are all eliminated."

"Yes." Changó sighed. "Oshun will end up writing a check that she can't cash." He frowned. "Or something like that."

"I don't think the humans say it like that, but I get your point. I know how crazy Oshun can be. I was married to her too, remember?"

The two *orisha* shared a masculine laugh before Changó flashed out of the forest. Erinle walked further downstream to a favorite copse of herbs, deep in thought. He'd sensed something in Violet when he healed her, something that he needed to keep an eye on, something that he didn't mention to neither Changó nor Oyá . If what he suspected was true, then there was more trouble coming indeed. And Oshun wouldn't be placated this time.

STORMBRINGER

If you enjoyed Stormbringer, then check out this excerpt from *Ironborn* (Orisha Rising #2)

Christian "C-Ted" Theodore sank yet another shot from the imaginary free throw line. After playing twenty years in the NBA for the Alaska Malamutes, one would think he'd had his fill of anything resembling a basketball. But since he'd retired at the end of the most recent season, he found that he still needed some sort of low-key connection to the game. Which was why he was on the playground at seven in the morning, making free throws. Granted, he had a full-sized, regulation NBA court in the basement of his home in Sandy Springs, Georgia, but he liked the playground; it reminded him of his humble beginnings on a small island in the Caribbean, when no one had even heard of him. The locals didn't even come to see him and his friends play.

The ball fell without effort through the net as he thought about Violet Davidson. To say that she was surprised to be partnered with him during his private aikido training sessions was an understatement. What he didn't understand was the undercurrent of resentment he'd picked up

from her, though she tried to hide it. It had
been obvious that she wasn't particularly thrilled
that he was going to be practicing at the dojo;
had it not been for the *sensei*'s request, he
doubted that she'd have agreed to train him
privately to bring him up to speed. She didn't
even bat an eye when he'd mentioned payment,
so he guessed that money wasn't a motivating
factor.

Although he shouldn't be too puzzled; she
probably thought that he was just using his
notoriety to garner special favors from *sensei*,
like private workout time. Or that he purchased
favor with some sort of donation to the dojo. He
was used to people assuming such things; it
came with the territory of being a professional
athlete.

Granted, his money and fame made some
things easier, but he'd never stopped working for
what he had. He'd been exposed to various
martial arts styles for years as part of his
professional training regimen, but it had been a
mixed bag of various *kata* cobbled together from
different disciplines. He'd never stuck with any
particular style. His personal trainer had
introduced elements of aikido during his last
playing season, and Christian loved it. He decided

to concentrate on that particular discipline after he retired, when he could really focus on earning his *kyu*. The thought of starting at the white-belt level at the grand age of forty was amusing. Maybe he could get his kids to take classes with him too, although his daughter was fast approaching the age where she would be embarrassed to be seen with him in public.

He sighed as he dribbled the ball and squared up to make a shot.

Swish. The ball floated through the rickety iron rim just as a crack of lightning flashed in the distance, followed by a peal of thunder. Christian looked at the steel-colored sky and sniffed the air; he could smell the rain, and it was going to fall pretty soon. No sooner than he'd finished that thought, fat droplets fell with increasing speed. He tucked the ball beneath his arm and dashed as fast as his surgically repaired knee would allow to his SUV.

He sat in his car until the storm subsided. He'd always liked thunderstorms, especially the lightning; when he was a child, back home on the island, he would stay in the rain until his mother made him come into the house. The rains were cooler--and more polluted-- here in the States, so standing in it wasn't the smartest move. Still, the water drumming on the roof of his truck was soothing. He waited until the downpour slowed to a light patter and drove to his favorite grocery store. He needed to pick up spaghetti makings, per his children's request.

Christian ducked his head to avoid hitting it on the doorway as he entered the brightly lit store. He made a beeline for the juice bar. He completed his shopping while sipping on a mango-coconut-pineapple smoothie with a protein boost; he only had to pose twice for a selfie with other customers, which was tantamount to going incognito for him. While searching for a particular brand of frozen garlic bread--his eight year-old son would eat no other kind--a voice floated over his shoulder.

"Find everything you're looking for, sir?"

Christian turned and saw a woman standing in front of his half-filled cart. He didn't have to look too far down to reach her sparkling brown eyes; since he was almost seven feet tall in his bare feet, that was saying something.

"Uh, yeah. I got everything on my list. Thank you." He tossed the garlic bread into his basket and glanced at the woman from beneath his eyelashes. Something about her seemed familiar, but he could have sworn that he'd never seen her before; not at this store, anyway. She was easy on the eyes and combined with her height, he would have remembered her.

The woman grinned, displaying even, white teeth that rivaled her eyes for the sparkle factor. Her hair was twisted into a crown of neat dreadlocks atop her head, making her seem even taller. He noticed that she carried a clipboard but didn't have a name tag affixed to her purple blouse, which meant she was probably in store management. "We appreciate your business, Mr. Theodore. You have a nice day, now."

Christian nodded his thanks and wheeled his cart to the checkout line. He didn't see the brief flash of light as the woman disappeared.

***

Oyá reappeared in the world of the *orisha* and walked to the great hut that was the home of Olorun, the Wise Father manifestation of one-third of the Supreme Creator trilogy of Olodumare/Olorun/Olofi. She entered the entrance to the hut and knelt. "*Baba*," she greeted.

"Rise, Oyá," Olorun replied. The Wise Father sat at a large wooden table, staring down into a great bowl filled with water. His white robes were shot through with gold thread that glittered in the rays of the sunlight that shone through a nearby window.

Oyá did so, then nodded to the other *orisha* that sat on a low three-legged stool nearby. "Eshú."

"Mother of Nine," Eshú winked. He puffed on a pipe; the fragrant scent of tobacco mixed not unpleasantly with the incense that Olorun burned all the time.

"Come." Olorun waved Oyá closer.

Oyá took measured steps, the nine panels of her rag skirt fluttering with each stride. When she was close enough she said, "I have made contact, *Baba*."

Olorun shot her a sharp glance. "And?" Eshú looked on with great interest from his stooled perch.

"He is of my lineage." The palm fronds of her mask trembled with each syllable she spoke.

Olorun looked back into the scrying bowl with a frown. "What of the man's father?"

Oyá sighed heavily, pushing the palm fronds out enough to grant a glimpse of her full lips. "I sensed Ogún's energy there."

Eshú cackled. "Ogún the righteous, who was against the *omo sonu olorun* from the very beginning. So he has succumbed to temptation as well."

"It wouldn't be the first time," Oyá retorted. Ogún was her ex-husband; when she left him for the mighty *orisha* Changó, Ogún sought solace in the arms of her sister Oshun. Of course, one could argue that it was only fair since Changó was Oshun's husband at the time, but Oyá was in no mood to be conciliatory.

Olorun raised a hand and the other two *orisha* fell silent. He pondered the scrying bowl as he addressed Oyá. "Are you certain the man is of Ogún's lineage as well?"

"I believe so, *Baba*, but I cannot know for sure. I can only be certain of my own lineage."

"I will go and tell him," Eshú said as he rose. He adjusted the red and black beaded necklace that clacked against his red robes.

"No," Olorun countermanded. "Let Oyá do it."

Oyá removed her mask, revealing a beautiful brown face with large brown eyes that reflected her surprise. "*Baba*?" Eshú stared at Olorun as well, the stem of his pipe hanging from his surprise-slackened mouth.

"It would be better coming from you. Besides, you know how Ogún gets into his moods. He may very well try to hurt Eshú for simply relaying information, and then I'd have to punish him. No one wants that. You can handle him."

Oyá nodded as she fingered the hilt of one of the machetes that hung at her sides. Ogún had forged both swords for her as a gift on their wedding day. She had used it countless times when she fought beside Ogún in a battle, and later when she fought beside Changó. The blades were sharp and swift, and the hilts molded to her hands like possessive lovers. They were one of best things that Ogún had ever given her. "As you wish, *Baba*."

"Go now."

Oyá bowed and left the hut. Once she'd gone, Olorun turned a troubled gaze upon Eshú. "This is the third of the Lost Children's descendants to manifest on earth."

"Third? We know of Oyá's descendant Violet; who was the second?"

"We suspect a human woman who is in service to Oshun. But Oshun has kept this a secret, and Erinle altered the woman's memories to the point that she may not even remember her powers."

"But the human man's powers haven't manifested, *Baba*. How could Oyá know?"

"He is a very gifted human athlete. He plays what they call basketball, and is apparently very famous."

"Ah, basketball." Eshú nodded. "A game that is well suited for very tall humans. They put a ball through a hoop that is well off the ground, and they get points for doing so. The team with the most points wins. It is a very lucrative profession in the human realm." He shifted on his stool. "Oyá does enjoy looking out for all types of athletes."

"Indeed. But I wonder at Ogún's energy there?"

"Would you like me to find out more, *Baba*?

"Yes. Observe this human male and see if he is manifesting any of Ogún's powers. Let me know; I want to know how he should be protected, should Ogún fail to see reason."

Eshú bowed before he rose from his stool once more. "As you wish, *Baba*."

IRONBORN, the second in the Orisha Rising series
Release date: January 2016

STORMBRINGER

FEATURED ORISHA

☐ **Aganjú (Aggayú)**: god of volcanoes and deserts. Husband of Yemajá. Father/brother of Changó. Sacred color: brown. Sacred number: 9

☐ **Babalúayé (Sopona)**: god of healing. Rules infectious diseases and skin ailments. Sacred colors: white, brown, blue, black. Sacred number: 17

☐ **Changó (Shangó)**: god of thunder, fire and war. Rules drums, music, power, male sexuality. One of the four major (pillar) *orisha*. Son of Yemajá. Son/brother of Aganjú. Husband of Oba and Oshun. Lover/husband of Oyá. Sacred colors: red and white. Sacred number: 6

☐ **Erinle (Inle)**: god) of healing, physical health and wellness. Can take male or female form. Lover of Yemajá. Husband of Oshun. Brother of Ochosi and Osain. Sacred colors: yellow, turquoise blue, red, green, pink. Sacred number:

☐ **Eshú (Legba/Eleggua/Exu)**: god of the crossroads and doorways. Rules communication and connection. Known as the trickster. Messenger between humans and the *orisha*. One-third of the *orisha* (along with Ochosi and Ogún) known as the *guerrero* (The Warriors). Sacred colors: red and black. Sacred number: 3, 21

- ☐ **Ibeji**: the sacred twins. Gods of happiness, play, abundance, laughter. Individuals in human form, but one *orisha*. Children of Changó and Oshun. Can appear as same sex or male/female twins. Sacred colors: red and blue. Sacred numbers: 2, 4, 8.

- ☐ **Oba (Obba)**: first and banished wife of Changó. Ruler of marriage and personal transformation. Sister of Yemajá, Oshun, and Oyá. Sacred colors: brown, coral, opal. Sacred number: 8

- ☐ **Obatala**: god of spiritual and moral uprightness. One of the four major (pillar) *orisha*. Son of Olorun. Father/husband of Yemajá. Father of Oba, Oyá, and Oshun. Sacred color: white.

- ☐ **Ochosi (Oxosi)**: god of hunting. Rules justice, law, police officers. Brother of Erinle and Osain. Brother/best friend of Ogún. One-third of the *orisha* (along with Eshú and Ogún) known as the *guerrero* (The Warriors). Sacred colors: blue and amber. Sacred numbers: 3 and 7

- ☐ **Ogún (Ogoun)**: god of metal. Rules battle, transportation, construction, surgeons, engineers, and soldiers/police/law enforcement. Son of Obatala. Husband/lover of Oshun. Possible brother of Osain and Changó. One-third of the *orisha* (along with Eshú and Ochosi) known as the *guerrero* (The Warriors). Sacred colors: green and black. Sacred number: 3

- [ ] **Olodumare**: The Supreme Creator of all *orisha* and one-third of the creator trinity that includes Olorun and Olofi. Female *orisha*.

- [ ] **Olofi:** Ruler of the earth. One-third of the creator trinity that includes Olodumare and Olorun.

- [ ] **Olokun**: god of the sea, especially the depths where light does not easily reach. Can be considered male or female. Does not often appear in human form. Father of Yemajá. Sacred colors: dark blue and green. Sacred number: 9

- [ ] **Olorun**: one-third of the creator trinity of Olodumare, the Supreme Creator. Olorun is the wise counsel and father figure.

- [ ] **Orunmila (Orunla/Orula/Ifá)**: god of wisdom, divination, and prophecy. Husband of Yemajá and Oshun. Sacred colors: yellow and green/brown and green. Sacred number: 16

- [ ] **Osain (Osanyin)**: god of healing, wild plants, magic. Rules the forest and all plants. Brother of Erinle and Ochosi. Godfather of Changó. Possible brother of Ogún. Sacred colors: green, red, white, yellow. Sacred numbers: 7 and 21

- [ ] **Oshun (Osun/Ochun/Oxun)**: goddess of beauty, love and sensuality. Rules rivers and streams. One of the four major (pillar) *orisha*. Sacred color: yellow. Sacred number: 6

☐ **Oyá (Yansa)**: goddess of storms. Rules storms, lightning, wind, change, ancestors (Egun), the marketplace. Protector of the cemetery. Lover/second wife of Changó. Younger sister of Yemajá, elder sister of Oshun. Sacred colors: purple, maroon. Sacred number: 9

☐ **Yeguá (Yewa)**: goddess of death. Rules the dead, death, the dying process, and the underworld. Sacred color: pink.

☐ **Yemajá (Yemoja/Yemaya)**: goddess of oceans and deep bodies of water. Also rules fertility. One of the four major (pillar) *orisha*. Elder sister of Oshun and Oyá. Mother of Changó. Wife of Aganjú an Obatala. Daughter of Olokun. Lover of Erinle (Inle) and Ogún. Sacred colors: blue and white. Sacred number: 7.

GLOSSARY (Yoruba)

aja -- dog (derogatory term)

Aruwo-Ara -- thunder

Baba -- father

Iya -- mother

Omo sọnu olorun (Yoruba) -- loosely translated, "the lost children of the gods"

STORMBRINGER

ABOUT THE AUTHOR

Tai Daniels is the pen name of a cult-favorite fiction author. She writes speculative fiction and cites Octavia Butler, Anne McCaffrey, Nalo Hopkinson, and Terry Brooks among her favorite authors. A graduate of Georgetown University, she resides in the Atlanta, GA area.

> Web: tiffscribes.com
> Twitter: @tiffscribes
> Instagram: tiffscribes
> Blog: tiffscribes.wordpress.com
> Facebook: facebook.com/tiffscribes

www.ingramcontent.com/pod-product-compliance
Lightning Source LLC
Chambersburg PA
CBHW021105130626
46554CB00002B/541